RETURN TO TORQUILLAN

Whilst working in Kenya, Alison Evans's husband, Clive, had disappeared without trace on a safari trip. Now, a year later, Alison has returned with her young daughter, Sophy, to the village of her birth, Torquillan, in the Scottish Highlands. When she takes a job at a marine biology station, Alison and her boss, Keir McMaster, become very attracted to each other. But Alison must find out what has happened to Clive before she can commit herself to another man.

Books by Ravey Sillars
in the Linford Romance Library:

THEIR ISLAND OF DREAMS
STRANGERS IN ACHNACRAIG
HIS BROTHER'S KEEPER

RAVEY SILLARS

RETURN TO TORQUILLAN

Complete and Unabridged

LINFORD
Leicester

First published in Great Britain in 1992

First Linford Edition
published 2003

British Library CIP Data

Sillars, Ravey
    Return to Torquillan.—Large print ed.—
    Linford romance library
    1. Love stories
    2. Large type books
    I. Title
    823.9'14 [F]

    ISBN 0–7089–4982–7

Published by
F. A. Thorpe (Publishing)
Anstey, Leicestershire

Set by Words & Graphics Ltd.
Anstey, Leicestershire
Printed and bound in Great Britain by
T. J. International Ltd., Padstow, Cornwall

This book is printed on acid-free paper

Arrival In Torquillan

'We're here, Sophy! We've arrived!' Alison Evans switched off the engine and glanced at her small daughter. Seven-year-old Sophy was flopped over her seat-belt fast asleep.

Alison's throat tightened, thinking how vulnerable her daughter looked — how delicate. The long journey had exhausted her. How on earth would she settle in this remote village, so far from all she knew and with only one of her parents?

Sudden, unexpected tears threatened Alison's brittle calm as she eased her stiff limbs out of the car.

The breeze struck her like a shower of ice. She had forgotten how cold March could be in the Highlands. The snow-clad hills that ringed Torquillan chilled the air.

She turned reluctantly from the cold

1

allure of the mountains as the setting sun began to edge them with gold. It was getting late.

Inside the house they must have heard their arrival for the door opened and her Uncle Sandy appeared on the doorstep, his eyes bright with astonishment.

'Alison! Alison, lass!' As Sandy Matheson held out his arms, she ran to him and was enfolded in a warm embrace.

'Where have you sprung from? Not driven all the way from the south?' he asked in disbelief.

She pulled out of his arms to answer.

'In stages. Didn't you get my letter?'

'No.' He shook his head. 'Peggy and I are just back today. She's only now away over to the post office for the mail.'

Alison nodded. 'I just knew you hadn't got it! I rang and rang, but I couldn't reach you.'

In fact she had been worried that Sandy and his sister would be away when she arrived in Torquillan.

'We were away on a trip with the Archaeological Society. But come in — come in till I see you! Leave the bairn a minute if she's sound.'

He put a comforting arm round her as he led her inside and guided her towards the living room.

'You've had a terrible time, lass. Is there no word of Clive yet? How long is it now? He was on a safari trip, wasn't he?'

'Yes. In Kenya. It's — it's almost a year since he disappeared.' Alison was surprised to find her voice unsteady, for she had almost come to terms with the shock of her husband's mysterious disappearance. But the deep sympathy in her uncle's voice had almost broken her fragile composure.

It was weariness that made her vulnerable. Her shoulders drooped and she had to stifle an unexpected sob when, to her horror, she realised that there was someone unfamiliar in the living room.

Gulping and straightening her shoulders, she gave her uncle a reproachful look. Someone was reclining on the window-seat, long legs stretched out in front of him in an attitude of easy relaxation.

Sandy hastily introduced them. 'This is Keir McMaster, Alison — Keir, my niece, Alison Evans. She's just dropped in out of the blue!'

The long legs unfolded and a tall, athletic-looking man rose.

'How do you do, Mrs Evans,' he murmured.

His back was to the glow of the evening sky and she couldn't discern his features.

Thrown off balance by a stranger's presence, Alison suddenly wanted to get away.

'I'd better go and check on Sophy,' she faltered. 'She may have woken up.'

Sandy Matheson squared his shoulders. 'We'll carry her in and put her on the sofa. How big is she now?'

'She's seven, but still slight. I'll get her.'

'Keir could help . . . ' Sandy suggested.

'No, no — I'll manage.'

She felt that since her unexpected — and rather emotional — entrance, the man's whole demeanour had expressed boredom and disapproval. She could do without his help.

To further discourage him, she announced that Sophy had brought her cat, Tabitha, with her, too.

'She wouldn't be parted from her.'

She knew she was babbling, and as she dithered, the man was on his feet and preceding her outside, so that, nerves taut, aware of her unreasonable antagonism towards him, she was obliged to follow in his wake.

She leaned in the driver's door and unfastened Sophy's seat-belt and Keir McMaster scooped up the unresisting child and carried her inside as though she'd been made of air.

There was no sound from the

5

cat-basket on the back seat and Alison decided to deal with Tabitha's release later. She had no idea if they would be staying even one night at Tigh na Mara. That would depend on Aunt Peggy.

★　★　★

Keir McMaster had not resumed his seat but stood in the centre of the room, to Alison's eyes powerful and striking.

'Sit down, Keir,' Sandy urged. 'Sit down till we hear what's brought Alison up to the wilds. Not that she needs a reason to come and see her uncle . . . ' He turned an indulgent smile on his niece. 'You just needed to come and see us when you were troubled. Isn't that right, lass?'

Keir's dark eyes flicked towards Alison and she felt herself appraised with detachment.

'I'll not stay just now, Sandy,' he protested, and she felt uncomfortable, knowing she wasn't at her best, her auburn hair tousled, her clothes creased from the journey.

'Must you go, Keir?' His years as captain of several cruise ships had polished Sandy's easy manner with folk. 'We haven't even had a dram.'

He turned to Alison. 'Sit down by the fire, lass. Peggy shouldn't be long. Keir's just been telling me his news,' he went on. 'D'you know his bosses have had the gall to ignore his recommendation for an assistant at the marine biology station — and foisted some woman from the south on him!'

Alison sat down abruptly as her stomach clenched with a painful jerk. Colour rushed into her cheeks.

'That's me!' she whispered.

Sandy swivelled round to stare at her in astonishment.

'You?' he said helplessly. 'I knew you were in marine biology, or zoology, or whatever. I remember you were always drawing the dashed things. But I thought you were a kind of marine-life artist or some such.'

Keir McMaster's strongly-marked brows climbed as he turned his sardonic gaze on her.

'I have done illustrations for the work . . .' she stammered nervously. She knew she was stalling, while McMaster continued to look grimly at her.

Just then, Sophy woke, and as she looked about her in puzzlement, Alison rose thankfully and went to her. She drew her close to her side, murmuring soothingly, and when next she looked round, the men had gone.

At that moment Peggy was tip-toeing into the house with the mail. She had seen the unfamiliar car outside and, thus alerted to visitors, was hoping to avoid them. There was always a constant stream of callers wanting Sandy's help or advice and she was forever having to make cups of tea.

Cautiously she opened the living room door only to find her brother alone, standing with his back to the fire, deep in thought.

'Who's here?' she whispered conspiratorially, sliding round the door and closing it softly behind her.

'I've got a fine surprise for you, Peggy.' Sandy lifted his head and made a beckoning gesture. 'Alison's here! Alison and wee Sophy! Isn't that grand?'

'Why are they here?' A number of expressions chased across Peggy's face: surprise, curiosity and finally a trace of hostility.

'Do they need a reason?' Sandy's thick brows descended. 'As a matter of fact, Alison's the new assistant at the research station.'

★　★　★

Peggy sat on the edge of a chair, her back rigid.

'Where will they stay?'

'I've said they can have the flat.'

'I thought you said the flat was mine if I wanted it!' Peggy protested.

9

'Well, you've never moved in, have you?'

'It's not very convenient — and it's full of . . . '

'Your junk. It can be cleared out,' Sandy said decisively.

'It's not junk — ' she began, but just then the door opened and Alison appeared.

'Aunt Peggy!' she cried. 'I didn't hear you come in!'

She crossed the room and gave a dutiful kiss to her aunt's stiff and unyielding cheek. Although Peggy resembled Alison's mother in appearance, she was very different in temperament.

She still held the letters, clutched like a shield against her chest.

'There's a letter from you here, Alison,' she said in a tone that was almost accusing.

'Yes. Obviously I meant you to get it earlier than this, before we arrived. It's to tell you about the job and asking if you know of any house we might rent.'

'Well, you don't have to worry about that any more.' Sandy sat down beside the fire. 'You'll be fine with us till the flat's ready.'

'It's a bad time of year to get anything to let with the season coming on. Nearly Easter.' Peggy lowered the letters to her lap. 'What made you apply for a job away up here?'

'Wheesht, Peggy.' Her brother shook his head at her. 'Where would she go but here? This is home for Alison while her parents are away abroad. We'll get Gavin Dunbar round to give us a hand clearing the flat.'

'Is Gavin back, then?' Alison asked.

'Ay. I remember you and he were very thick those summers when your mother used to bring you here for holidays.'

Alison nodded. 'We used to have great fun. Is he married now?'

'Not him!. He's still staying with his mother. He's a forest ranger now, you know, and takes a great interest in all the flora and fauna round about.'

'He seems to have more interest in girls if you ask me,' Peggy added sharply.

'Och, Peggy. There's nothing wrong with the lad. And his mother and me are the best of friends.'

'How did the flat come about, Uncle Sandy?' Alison tried to change the subject.

'The end room was once a stable, and what we call the flat used to be stable lofts. And a very handy conversion it's proved to be for the times when the family comes home.'

'Aah! What's that!' Peggy let out a screech as a grey and black striped cat came out from under the sofa. 'Get away! Get away!' she squealed, flapping the letters at the animal which shot in panic to the door.

'How did that get in?' she demanded.

Nervous colour ran into Alison's cheeks.

'I'm sorry, Aunt Peggy — I didn't mean her to get in here. She's Sophy's cat. I'll try to keep her out of the way.'

'She can't stay here!' Peggy snapped.

'Peggy doesn't care for cats,' Sandy added unnecessarily as Alison went in pursuit of the animal.

When she'd got Tabitha out of the way, Alison remembered why she had come downstairs in the first place.

'I've given Sophy some supper and left her getting undressed for her bath. I came to ask if I could borrow a towel?'

'They're in the chest on the landing. Help yourself,' said her aunt, graciously recovering. 'Is the room warm enough?'

'We've seen to everything,' her brother assured her.

★ ★ ★

Sophy's tired-looking rag doll was already in her bed in the guest room.

'Hurry and get in beside Belinda,' Alison coaxed, 'she'll be lonely.'

Sophy clung to her suddenly. 'Mummy, don't leave me!' The child's eyes were huge and pleading. 'Everything's so strange . . .'

13

'I know, love, but you'll soon settle in. What you're needing is a good sleep and then in the morning we can go exploring and it won't seem strange any more.'

Sophy climbed reluctantly into bed.

'Will some other little girl be getting into my bed at home, Mummy?' she asked as Alison tucked her in.

'Yes, pet, I told you that. Another little girl is going to be using your room for a while. But all your toys and books are on their way here.'

The child looked soothed, and Alison perched on the edge of bed and touched her forehead gently.

'Time to go to sleep now, pet,' she murmured.

As the little girl obediently closed her eyes, Alison thought of the house they'd just left behind.

It had been more Clive's house than hers — everything had been to his taste. Well, it had been Clive's money and he had enjoyed spending it. She'd been very busy looking after Sophy and studying, so she had been content to leave him to furnish their home.

She smiled wryly. Her father, Colonel Guy McKenzie, had only agreed to the marriage on the condition that she promised to complete her degree, but she would have promised anything to marry Clive!

However, she was grateful now for that stern discipline, for it enabled her to earn a living now.

Clive had earned a lot — and spent a lot. The house, the furnishings, the foreign holidays, the sports car — they had all been paid for by him. But he had been self employed — as an oil engineer — which meant there had been no money since he'd disappeared. No life insurance either, as there was no proof he was dead.

So she had had to become the breadwinner. Things weren't easy. She'd have liked to sell the car and buy a smaller one which was cheaper to run, but she was afraid he might come home and want his car, his house, his child, his wife . . .

Sophy had fallen fast asleep and Alison looked down at her with a worried frown.

'Oh, Sophy, please like it here!' she whispered. 'I simply had to get away. I couldn't stand that house and all its memories any more!'

A Cool Reception

'But, darling! There's never been anyone but you!' he protested. 'I want to believe you . . . ' Marie Blair raised herself on one elbow on the couch, letting her kimono slip daringly off her shoulders, 'but how can I — after all that's happened?'

'Believe me, my love . . . ' he murmured.

'Stop!' the director yelled. 'Put a bit of passion into it, Gavin! It's a farce — not a wake!'

'Well, for heaven's sake, I'm only doing it to help you out!'

'He doesn't look right for the part in any case.' Marie's long-lashed violet eyes opened wide. 'He should have dark hair and grey eyes.'

'You mean I'm not Dr McMaster?' Gavin snorted. 'Get Keir McMaster to do the part of Jeremy then.' He jumped nimbly from the stage on to the hall floor. 'I'm not dyeing my hair for anybody!'

'Now, you two, that's enough!' the director said placatingly. 'It's less than a month till the festival. Get back on the stage, Gavin, and take it from the beginning of the scene.'

Gavin obliged, and the rehearsal passed without any more incident until they broke for a welcome cup of tea half an hour later.

'Phew, I'm parched!' Marie threw back her mane of curly hair and sipped delicately at her tea.

Perched on a table, while the rest of the cast sat around on chairs, she looked like a star surrounded by her satellites. She was, everyone acknowledged, uncommonly attractive. And the excitement of acting seemed always to heighten her charisma and make her glow. There was no doubt that she had star quality.

With rare philosophy, Gavin was thinking that she was quite a large fish in the small pond that was Torquillan. Nevertheless, he liked pretty girls, and he had every intention of walking her home after the rehearsal.

The second half of their rehearsal elicited little more approval from the director who finally threw up his hands in disgust and sent them all home early.

Like children let out of school, nine of the drama club swarmed into McDonald's Hotel at the head of the quay. Donald McDonald was a kindly man with time to listen to his patrons, and when they arrived, he was leaning over the bar deep in conversation with Keir McMaster.

Marie's eyes lit up and, leaving the others, she approached the two men with dancing steps.

'Keir — just the person we're looking for! We're needing new blood in our play. How would you like to take over the male lead from Gavin . . . opposite me?'

McMaster turned slowly from his discussion with Donny and raised a quizzical eyebrow.

'Juvenile lead?' he queried. 'I'm too old!'

'No, you're not!' Marie protested and slipped an arm through his. 'Come and join us,' she pleaded. 'Come and hear all about it.'

'I'm busy just now — I'm talking to Donald. I'll talk to you later,' he promised dismissively.

With that she had to be content, and she tripped back to join the rest of the drama group, where Gavin's scowl was becoming ominous.

★　★　★

Gavin Dunbar was about to climb into his pick-up outside the house two mornings later when he spotted Alison, who was taking Sophy along to see the head teacher at the primary school.

'Alison! Alison McKenzie — I mean Evans!'

He threw his haversack into the vehicle and sprinted after her as she turned to see who was calling her name.

As he reached her he swept her off her feet in a warm embrace and smacked a kiss on to her cheek.

'Great to see you!' he cried, then looked down at Sophy, watching the scene curiously. 'Is this your daughter?'

'Yes. This is Sophy. She's seven.'

'Are you off to school?' he asked the girl encouragingly.

'Yes,' she answered. She looked pale and tired and a little worried, he noted.

'Don't worry about it!' Gavin smiled at her. 'I went to that school when I was wee, and it's very nice. Not too big. Not too many people to get to know. I'll introduce you to my sister's little girl if you like. She's about your age.'

He pushed to the back of his mind the thought that she might, with her English accent and her fragile looks, be treated as an outsider.

He turned back to Alison.

'Sandy phoned,' he told her. 'I was out, but Mum took the message. I'll be round tonight to help clear out the flat for you. I'll dress as a furniture remover,' he added, and as Alison laughed, to Gavin it sounded an echo of the carefree girl he had once known.

'I heard about — your husband,' he said awkwardly. 'I'm sorry. It's an awful thing.'

'Yes.' A look of strain instantly shadowed her eyes and he wished he hadn't said anything.

'How about going to Donny's for a wee while later on?' he said quickly, trying to lighten the mood again. 'I'd enjoy a blether about old times. D'you remember — you were once my best girl?'

'How could I forget? We used to have great fun, didn't we? The old crowd! The seasonal jobs, the summer dances! But it's all so long ago. Things have changed.' She gave an involuntary sigh.

'Never mind!' he told her bracingly. 'The good Torquillan air will buck you up! See you tonight then?'

'Yes, all right. Thanks, Gavin. It's good — good to be back.'

Gavin was whistling as he returned to his truck, while Alison swung Sophy's hand as they resumed their walk to school.

'He's a nice man, Mum.' Sophy looked up into her mother's face. 'And he's got hair like mine!'

'Not quite your colour. But he is nice, Sophy. And he's coming round tonight to help us get the flat ready.'

'Will he tuck me up, do you think, the way Daddy used to?'

'He might, darling. I'm sure he will if you ask him.'

Alison's throat tightened. Poor Sophy still missed her daddy so much. How was she going to cope with all the other changes that lay ahead for her?

★ ★ ★

Alison's apprehension increased the following Monday as she approached the marine research station to start her

23

new job and confront Keir McMaster — her new boss.

She knew she had to make a success of this job — there was no turning back.

She'd seen the advertisement for a research assistant at Torquillan by chance. From the vantage point of her hectic life in the south, Torquillan had seemed to beckon — a haven for herself and Sophy — far from all reminders of Clive.

When she'd got word that the job was hers, it had seemed like a heaven-sent opportunity to make a fresh start. She had given up her good job working on experimental oyster-farming programmes near Colchester, had sub-let the house — and here she was.

The marine station came in sight. It was fairly new and still developing. At present it was a long, E-shaped concrete building, housing, she knew from the information she'd been sent, a museum, a library, an aquarium, laboratories, offices, sorting and packing rooms. It had brought much-needed work to the area, employing local people as scientific assistants, lab technicians, cleaners, office staff, handymen and boat crew.

In front of the building a stone jetty jutted out into the sea, and moored at the end lay the station's boat, the Kelpie. As she glanced over she could see, proceeding towards it, carrying some scuba diving equipment, two young men with Keir McMaster.

He looked both impatient and undecided when he caught sight of her, increasing her wariness of him. He seemed to make a decision, spoke to the other two, who went on without him, and retraced his steps towards her.

All she needed was courage, Alison told herself.

'Good morning! Lovely day!' she greeted him, her voice expressing more confidence than she felt.

'I forgot you were starting this morning,' he admitted, sighing.

Well, of course, you would, she thought sourly.

'I'd better show you round,' he added less than graciously, so that Alison was sure he felt it a painful duty when his heart was back on the boat and he would far rather be preparing to dive into the clear green water on this unexpectedly sparkling morning.

With an outward show of calm acceptance, she accompanied him into the station building.

'If you'll just wait here till I change, please . . .'

He showed her into a small office. Here Marie Blair was sitting in front of a word processor, studying hand-written notes with a puzzled frown.

'Marie Blair — Alison Evans, my new assistant,' he introduced them briefly, then disappeared.

Left together, Alison sat down and gave the other girl a friendly smile.

'You'll be the secretary here? Do you enjoy the work?'

'Yes, but — the words!' Marie

wrinkled her nose and pointed at the note she was trying to decipher. 'Are there supposed to be two i's in euphausiids?'

'Yes.' Alison laughed, and they didn't speak again as Marie went back to work.

Keir returned presently and ushered Alison out of the room.

'We'll start with the museum. Along with the aquarium, it's open to the public and we like to feature special displays from time to time. Perhaps you'd like to prepare one on the life-cycle of oysters?'

She stopped, fascinated by a well-mounted exhibition of seaweeds, and sensed rather than saw the faint flicker of impatience in his eyes.

Her back stiffened.

'There's no need,' she told him crisply, 'for you to waste your valuable time showing me round. I can study this for myself. Or perhaps you could delegate someone less important to escort me?'

He studied her for a long moment in silence and she wondered if she had overstepped the mark.

'That might not be a good idea,' he said at last. 'Our museum attendant isn't here at present.'

He turned to indicate a large model in the middle of the room.

'This is a model of the area showing Loch Torlin. An oyster-farming experiment has been set up in the lochan which joins Loch Torlin. Your appointment is because of your experience in that field.'

'Yes, so I gather. I also gather from what my uncle said the other night that I'm not the assistant you wanted?'

A fleeting look of chagrin crossed his face but all he said was, 'Really?'

It was dismissive but Alison refused to be put off. It was better to clear the air now, she thought. If I'm to work here, I must know where I stand.

'You're not interested in oyster culture?' she hazarded.

'I'm not uninterested in oyster work.' His eyes narrowed on her. 'But I prefer the scientific staff, if possible, to be . . . '

She was almost certain he was going to say 'men', or 'unencumbered women', and laughed outright when he concluded, 'experienced divers,' so that he looked at her in astonishment.

Would she bother telling him that she possessed a good British Sub Aqua Club diving certificate? A qualification that had proved quite acceptable for diving outside Britain, too, when she'd dived in Spain, Malta and North Africa?

Alison shrugged, decided it would sound like point-scoring, and left her laughter unexplained.

'Through here,' he said, opening a door, 'is the aquarium for which the preserved exhibits in the museum are meant to be an introduction.'

It was cold and dark in the long, tank-lined room. The only light was a dim, greenish illumination, simulating underwater conditions for the numerous creatures living there.

Alison felt the old thrill of her calling when she observed the healthy marine life so brilliantly displayed. And yet, unreasonably, in spite of her fascination with the displays of living creatures, she wanted the tour to end.

She was aware of an uncomfortable sensation caused by this man's close proximity. She wanted to walk away and yet felt drawn to him. As they stood together in front of one of the tanks, a strange tension seemed to stretch between them and she found herself surreptitiously studying him.

She judged him to be about thirty-four, lean, his skin healthily tanned. His dark hair sprang back from his brow and his grey eyes had a steely gleam. He stood easily, his body still, long hands resting on the casing of the tank. At that moment, as if sensing her regard, he turned towards her, his narrow, guarded eyes inscrutable.

'Shall we continue?'

They soon completed the station tour and finished up in his office.

'I'll give you the papers on the oyster project to date,' he said as they entered the room.

He handed her a folder across the desk, indicating that she should sit down, and took his own seat. Here comes the interrogation, she thought.

However, it wasn't as bad as she feared. She was simply questioned on her past work before he turned to more personal matters.

'Have you made arrangements to have your daughter looked after when you're at work?' he asked.

'She's started school.'

'But she won't always be at school,' he pointed out.

'True. I have to finalise those arrangements.'

She didn't mention that quite what those arrangements would be, she didn't yet know. What she did know was that there was no point in asking Aunt Peggy to help — she'd never been very good with children.

'I see you're married,' Keir was continuing. 'There's no chance of you suddenly taking off to be with your husband? I don't like work to be disrupted for any reason.'

A cold hand seemed to clutch at her heart. What if Clive should, even at this late date, reappear? What if she should be suddenly obliged to drop everything and go to him? She daren't even mention such a possibility . . .

He seemed to be waiting for some final confirmation from her.

'My work will not be disrupted for any reason over which I have control,' she said carefully, and as she uttered the words, she wondered how much he knew of her circumstances. How much did he guess?

Through the window, behind his head, she could see the snow-topped mountain of Ben Dorn. She looked up at the great peak and then back at the hard angles of Keir McMaster's face, seeing the same chilly aloofness there.

It was obvious that there was no welcome for her here. Had she made the right decision in coming here? What did the future hold for her and Sophy in Torquillan?

Poor Sophy

It was after five-thirty before Alison was free to go home from the station.

She had just decided that she would drive to work in future, in order to get back quickly to Sophy, when she saw Gavin's pick-up speeding towards her.

'Get in!' he said tersely, braking beside her.

'What is it?' she asked as she climbed in.

'It's Sophy! My mother sent me to fetch you.' He quickly turned the pick-up and put his foot down.

'What's wrong? Is she hurt?' Her throat went dry.

'No. Mum said to tell you that she suddenly burst into tears more than an hour ago — and they can't get her to stop.'

Alison was aghast. 'But she never cries!'

'Maybe that's the trouble,' he observed. 'Anyway, Sandy phoned for Mum to go round to see if she could do anything with her.'

'Uncle Sandy was meeting Sophy from school,' Alison recalled.

'Yes. They all walked home together — Mum goes for Helen, my niece.'

When they reached the Mathesons' house, Alison was out of the pick-up and running indoors almost before Gavin had switched off the engine.

Sophy was sitting on the couch with Bess Dunbar on one side of her, and her great-uncle Sandy on the other, his hands hanging helplessly between his knees as the child sat sobbing inconsolably.

'Alison! Thank goodness!' Sandy rose, relinquishing his seat to her with a heartfelt sigh. 'I thought she'd do herself a mischief.'

Sophy's face was swollen with crying and tears were still coursing down her cheeks as she nestled into her mother's arms. Alison held her close and rocked her gently.

'It's all right. It's all right, Mummy's here. What's the matter, pet?'

'She seemed to be crying for 'Bunty',' Bess Dunbar put in quietly. 'But she couldn't tell us who that was.'

'Bunty was our daily help in Colchester,' Alison explained. 'She always looked after Sophy until I came home. They used to make the meal together, didn't you, darling? Has everything been too strange and new all at once?'

Oh, God, Alison was thinking, what have I done? I wanted to make a new life for myself and Sophy — but have the changes been too much for her?

She looked down at her daughter's brimming eyes, feeling the pain of responsibility for her distress, her own throat choking with tears of sympathy.

'Sophy, Sophy, please don't cry. Did something upset you, darling?'

Sophy shook her head in denial, but still she couldn't speak.

Alison didn't press her but just went on rocking her until, in time, and from exhaustion, the child's weeping began to subside.

Alison looked over Sophy's head to Bess Dunbar, and Sandy.

'Thank you both so much. I'm sorry you've had all this bother. This is just not like Sophy. She's normally such a plucky little thing!'

At that moment Sophy's cat, Tabitha, stalked into the room and leapt up beside her mistress.

'Tabitha!' Sophy whispered.

Everyone was relieved to hear Sophy's voice and see her stretch a hand out to the cat who promptly curled up beside her, and presently Sophy's eyelids began to droop.

Only a rogue sob or two more escaped her before she fell fast asleep with Tabitha's warm body purring against her side.

Bess Dunbar turned to her grand-daughter.

'Did anything happen at school to upset her?' she asked quietly.

Helen shook her head, making her

smooth brown hair bounce.

'Did she seem all right on the way home, Uncle Sandy?' Alison asked.

'Yes! Well . . . I didn't pay much heed. She and Helen walked ahead and Bess and I followed, having a natter.'

Alison frowned thoughtfully, gazing down at her sleeping daughter's soft golden curls.

'I told Keir McMaster that I was finalising the arrangements for having Sophy cared for after school — just before I get home from work. You said you knew someone, Uncle Sandy?'

Sandy chuckled. 'That's Bess!' He turned a slow, imploring, almost ardent gaze upon her. 'I thought — since you have Helen to collect anyway . . . ?'

Bess met his look candidly. 'I was going to suggest it.'

Alison turned to Gavin's mother, her eyes full of hope. She had known the Dunbars before Mr Dunbar had died. In her fifties now, Bess was just as pretty as she'd always been — and it was no wonder Sandy had always been sweet on her.

'Would you, Mrs Dunbar?' She felt almost light-headed with relief. 'I can't tell you how grateful I would be!'

'It's no problem,' Bess assured her. 'My daughter does reception work in one of the hotels from now till October, and I help by taking Helen after school. One more will be no trouble.'

'It would be a business arrangement,' Alison added diffidently, and saw Bess's face flush.

'I wouldn't know what to charge. And ... och, I wouldn't like to be taking anything.'

'I know what the going rate is,' Alison said firmly. 'It means so much to me, I'd like to feel that you'd be properly recompensed. I'll pay you weekly. And there's no one I'd rather leave Sophy with.' She smiled.

'Oh — well — if you insist,' Bess returned her smile, and then, after a pause, went on, 'How's the flat coming on?'

'There's still some work to be done

before we can move in,' Alison told her.

'It's been a bit neglected these last few years, Bess.' Sandy put in. 'Alison had the plumber and the electrician in, and, next week, we're hoping the painter will come. They're all busy with the hotels and guesthouses at this time of year, that's the trouble.'

With a satisfied glance at the still-sleeping Sophy, Bess made a move to go.

'I'd better be on my way. Don't worry about Sophy too much, Alison. A change of location can be unsettling. I remember Gavin bursting into tears once when he was a wee boy because we had taken him away to Oban — for what was meant to be a treat!' Bess gave her infectious chuckle.

'Did I hear my name?' Gavin had been keeping out of the way in the kitchen but now came into the room. 'Do you want a lift home, Mum?'

'Please, Gavin. Come on, Helen — time to go.'

She glanced down at Sophy once

more and sighed.

'Och, the wee soul!' she murmured compassionately. 'I'll look after her as I do Helen. It's what I do best. Isn't that right, Sandy?' She twinkled back at him as she reached the door.

'What's that, Bess?'

'Look after folk!' And a light laugh floated back to them as she hurried off.

'I'll come back later and see how Sophy is,' Gavin promised before he followed on his mother's heels.

* * *

'Well, Marie, what's kept you so late tonight?' Isa McPhail asked as she cast the tablecloth accurately across the table.

'Extra typing, Aunt Isa.'

Marie flopped into a chair beside her grandmother, Agnes, and kicked off her high-heeled shoes.

'You mean you were impressing the director with how hard-working you are?' Isa snorted.

41

Marie fluttered her long eyelashes.

'I don't have to. He knows!' she declared.

'Good! Then you won't mind showing me too by setting the table while I see to the fish?'

'Oh, but Aunt Isa, I'm tired.' Marie stretched luxuriously and wriggled her stockinged toes. 'I want to sit here and watch the news.' Her hand reached across for her grandmother's. 'How are you tonight, Gran?'

'I'm fine, I'm fine!' Agnes smiled and raised a brown, wrinkled hand to touch one of Marie's silver earrings. 'And the better for seeing you, bonny lass.'

Isa selected cutlery from the drawer and placed it on the table with a clash.

'You're not the only one that's tired!' she complained to her niece, then added, 'Well, what's new?'

'Mrs Evans started today at the station. She's quite young looking.' A furrow of curiosity puckered Marie's brow. 'What age would she be, Aunt Isa?'

A faint humour touched her aunt's eyes.

'Oh, she's elderly, Marie. She's ages with Gavin Dunbar. Twenty-six, would it be?'

'Mmm. She looks young to have that child.'

'She got married very young, I remember. Quite infatuated she was. How she fitted in having a baby with going on studying, I've no idea. Her husband was abroad a lot, too. Did you hear about him being missing?'

'Yes. It's weird, isn't it? What if you were never, ever to know, for the rest of your life, whether your husband was alive or dead? How would you go on?' Marie asked with rare sensitivity, and Isa shook her head sadly.

'Who knows, love.' She looked up from laying the table as a thought struck her. 'Marie, if you could learn all these marine terms, you could maybe train as a biologist. You could get a job in any marine research place, or even in a university department maybe.'

Marie screwed up her nose. 'But I don't want that. What I'd really love is to be an actress in a long-running TV serial,' she sighed.

'Huh! You and your drama!' scoffed Isa but Marie was unconcerned.

'That reminds me — I've got to hurry. I'm going out.'

'Not another rehearsal!' Isa protested. 'But you had three last week!'

'I know, but we're working on the costumes tonight.'

'So you come in here too exhausted to help me,' Isa commented scathingly, 'but you've energy enough to go to your pal's to sew costumes all night! Your mother sent you up here to help me, remember. You were lucky to get that job but you should still have time to help around the house. Your gran loves having you here but goodness knows what your mother would say if she saw you swanning off out most nights, never lifting a finger to help look after your gran . . .'

Marie's pretty face assumed a mutinous scowl.

'Well, if you don't want me here, I'll move out. I can easily get digs in the village,' she retorted, tossing her head.

'You'll do nothing of the sort, not while I'm responsible for you. I'm going to phone your mother.'

'If you do that, I'm moving out,' Marie threatened, and Isa gave a deep sigh.

'As if I hadn't enough without this . . . '

Marie flounced up and pushed her feet back into her shoes.

'I'm away. I don't want any tea.' And the door closed behind her with a sharp click.

Isa stood perfectly still, an expression of shocked dismay in her eyes.

'Oh, Mother — what have I done? It's that tongue of mine again, isn't it? And,' she wailed, 'what will I do with all that fish?'

But Mrs McPhail, listening to the television news, didn't hear her.

Isa had just lowered herself into a chair and sunk her head in her hands when her mother did speak.

'When can I have my tea, Isa?' she asked, apparently unaware of the scene that had just been played out.

Isa rose again, wiping tears from her eyes.

'I'll just get it for you now, Mother. It's a nice wee bit of haddock. But I'm not very hungry myself.'

★   ★   ★

'Have you had time to read the papers I gave you yesterday on the oyster-farming experiment, Mrs Evans?'

She had seen the white-clad figure approaching out of the corner of her eye but since all the science staff wore white lab coats, it was a moment before Alison realised who was standing beside her.

She looked up into dark, serious eyes.

'Yes, of course, Dr McMaster.' She swallowed a flicker of nervousness. 'And

46

the publications of the West Coast oyster work which I got from the library.'

'Including the Loch Ryan experiment?'

'Naturally.'

'Conscientious!' A thread of surprised amusement laced his voice, but she held back the sarcastic reply which was on the tip of her tongue.

'Well?' He turned his head with the hint of a disarming smile. 'What do you think of them?'

'I think I can improve on the results you have obtained so far.'

His eyebrows shot up and he gave a contemptuous snort, and she caught her breath sharply, but she refused to back down and met his challenging gaze without a flicker.

'A lot of work has gone into the scheme already,' he told her coldly. 'Perhaps you would care to elaborate on your proposal?'

She looked at his thinned lips and narrowed eyes. Was he more personally concerned in the experiment than he had cared to indicate?

For a moment she said nothing, but glanced along the bench to where one of the lab assistants was setting up a microscope. She didn't want to talk about it where they might be overheard.

Getting her meaning at once, Keir McMaster's fingers closed on her upper arm and he led her over to one of the window embrasures, while a shiver traced a jagged trail up her spine.

He released her then and stood looking out at the stormy sea, patiently waiting for her to speak.

'You appear to have two aims,' she said slowly, barely able to see his eyes in the shadow of the lowered brows. 'To encourage the growth of oysters to commercial size and quality — and to see if you can establish a healthy breeding pattern here.'

'Restore,' he corrected her. 'There was once a successful fishing ground in the loch.'

'Restore, then.' She allowed herself a

small sigh, and took a step away from him. It wasn't only the man's presence that made her uneasy, it was her own reaction to it.

'Since natural breeding has ceased, for whatever reason,' she went on, 'I read that you have imported young oysters and laid down new beds, but the results over the past two summers have not been good.'

'With your experience, you must know that it's still early days,' he commented.

'Granted, but I would like to inspect the floor of the lochan.'

They both glanced out of the window, taking in the grey sea lashing the beach and the heavy clouds obscuring the land.

'Not the best moment to suggest that!' he said sardonically.

Alison felt her stomach churn at his tone and she found it an effort to persist.

'Some questions worry me . . . ' She went on to outline them, concluding with a query about predators.

'Ah! Well,' he interrupted her with deceptive seriousness, 'that information I can provide. In addition to starfish and octopus, the traditional enemies, we have our own Loch Torlin monster!'

A sense of frustration swept over her. Oh, what was the use? It was impossible to communicate with this man!

Betraying none of her feelings, however, she merely shrugged coolly, though her heart was thumping.

'You know, of course, that the lochan is on the other side of the loch from here?' he went on in a more serious tone. 'The only reasonable way to approach it is by sea. To go round the head of the loch is a thirty-mile drive over winding, treacherous tracks.'

'Yes. I'm familiar with the area.' Her eyes were violet flames.

'So! We wait for the first good day and approach by boat?'

She nodded with apparent serenity.

'How do you propose to inspect the floor of the lochan?' he asked.

'I'll dive.'

She had the satisfaction of seeing his eyebrows jerk upwards.

'You didn't mention diving as one of your accomplishments on your application.'

'It wasn't stated as a necessary qualification for the job. And obviously it wasn't.'

'No. Quite . . . Well, we've set up a caravan laboratory as a field station near the site. You can take charge of the project from there. You'll be expected to stay up there in the summer and monitor the growth of the oysters and keep a watch on the breeding. You will also, of course, be anxious to keep a check on other conditions in the lochan.'

She wondered if he was getting some devilish kind of enjoyment out of the dilemma he was posing her.

'Yes,' she replied, dropping her eyelids to hide the smouldering fire in her eyes.

She had wanted to speak of her plans

to set up a hatchery here at the station, but she suddenly felt too exhausted by his opposition to pursue the topic any further.

He was impossible. He didn't want her here and he was obviously just trying to make life difficult for her. For how could she stay in a caravan on an inaccessible headland all summer, when she had a young daughter to look after?

★   ★   ★

'What are you doing, Sophy?' The teacher's voice was sharp. 'Not dreaming again?'

Sophy heard the class snigger.

'Quiet, everyone!' the teacher commanded, then looked again at Sophy. 'Sophy, please stand up.'

She rose to her feet, a dazed expression in her eyes.

'What were you doing, Sophy?' the teacher asked.

She didn't know. She couldn't remember anything before Miss Meikle had called to her.

She felt sick. She always felt sick — a little bit more every day.

Miss Meikle cast a stern glance over the rest of the class.

'Heads down, class! I'm coming round to inspect your writing in one minute!' Then she dropped her voice again and looked at Sophy. 'Sophy, come here, child.'

With dragging feet, she came down the passage between the desks to stand by the teacher's desk.

'Are you always so pale, child? Is there anything the matter?'

Miss Meikle's voice was low, but it was awful being picked out. People were peeking up at her secretly from their books, she could tell.

She wanted to say, 'I feel sick,' but how could she? They were all listening.

The sickness was coming anyway. Her mouth was filling with water and her forehead was getting colder and pricklier.

Putting her hand over her mouth she

ran out into the playground and was sick over a grating.

Through a kind of mist, she could see the boys jumping up to look out of the windows, then Miss Meikle was at her side.

'My goodness, dear — you're green!'

Miss Meikle put her arm round her and Sophy breathed in the scents of chalk and lily of the valley perfume. She would have liked to just stay there, nestling in the beige folds of Miss Meikle's cotton skirt for a while, but the other children were looking out of the window, so she pulled away.

'Come in now, pet.' The teacher's voice was kind. 'I'll phone your mother to come.'

'No!' Sophy felt a jolt of panic as she was led into the staff-room and placed in a chair beside the window that was thrown open. 'Mummy can't come.'

'Why not?' Miss Meikle asked as she gave her a glass of cold water.

'She works — at the station,' Sophy blurted out.

Miss Meikle nodded. 'At the marine station. I know. I'll phone there.'

'But she can't come!' Sophy protested. She didn't want to interrupt her mother's work, to be a nuisance to her.

The teacher studied her closely.

'Will I bring Helen to sit with you? Is Helen your best friend?'

She had to answer, 'Yes,' but she wasn't sure.

Helen had everything she wanted: brown eyes and hair, brown tanned skin and plump cheeks and arms and legs. Helen was beautiful — and everyone was her friend.

If only she herself hadn't been born skinny and pale, and not knowing the Gaelic that all the other children chattered in so naturally.

She was alone for a moment before Helen came in.

'This is great!' Helen plumped down on a chair and peeped into the teachers' biscuit tin. 'I'm glad you got me out of class.'

Her lovely brown, chubby legs with

their clean white socks and sandals swung back and forward, gently kicking the chair.

'It's nearly time to go home anyway. I said to Miss Meikle my granny would be here soon — and she would look after you.'

Meanwhile Sally Meikle was worried about Sophy and decided she should see her mother. Sophy just didn't seem to be settling in at all. So, she asked Alison to call at the school one evening.

After a few polite preliminaries, she came straight to the point.

'I'd like the child psychologist to see her, Mrs Evans,' she told Alison.

'A child ... Goodness! Is that necessary?' It sounded terribly serious, and Alison could feel the blood draining from her face. 'It's only three weeks ... '

'Nevertheless, I feel there's something amiss. Some children transplant well but Sophy doesn't seem to be adjusting as one would hope.'

'Her father ... ' Alison began, then

paused helplessly.

'Yes. I know.' The teacher smiled in sympathy. 'There is that . . . but it's been so long since she last saw him.' Sally Meikle's grave eyes looked at Alison steadily. 'Did you check with the doctor that day she was sick? I was wondering if it was nerves.'

Alison shrugged. 'The doctor couldn't tell. She prescribed some powders. I think they have the effect of calming as well as treating a gastric upset. Whatever it is they do, Sophy has seemed a lot better since then.' She knew her voice sounded relieved.

'Yes, that's true.' The teacher commented, then glanced down at Sophy's records on the desk. 'Her report from her last school is glowing. She's a clever little girl, but we're not seeing any evidence of it here.'

'I see,' Alison said, pushing her hair away from her forehead with a nervous gesture. She sent Sally Meikle a look that was both anxious and appealing. 'What can I do?'

The teacher considered the question — and the young woman sitting so taut and strained before her.

'Sometimes, in one-parent families, the parent is too anxious,' she suggested, then stopped when she saw the pain in Alison's face.

She closed the folder and pushed it aside, something in the gesture seeming to indicate a shelving of the matter.

'Look, the Easter holidays start on Friday. She can't be seen by the psychologist before then. I'll make an appointment for when we get back, shall I?'

'Yes, yes, all right.' Alison hesitated. 'And I'll try to be with her as much as I can during the holidays. I'll try to arrange some fun for her.'

Overwhelmed by feelings of inadequacy and guilt, and yet only too aware of the financial and emotional dilemma that had forced them on her, she said goodnight to the teacher and walked blindly from the school building and through the village.

*   *   *

Alison sat down heavily on a bench that overlooked the loch. It was April now and the day had been one of sunshine interspersed with heavy showers.

She recalled that Keir McMaster had been called away to the east coast to give advice on shellfish to a seminar there. Perhaps she could take Sophy to work with her while he was out of the way. She began to plan ways of amusing Sophy at the station while she got on with her work.

Her eyes focused again on the beauty of the scene and she caught her breath, wondering how she could have lived so long in cities.

She watched as a seal slid into the water, disturbing an oyster-catcher which excitedly started its loud piping call. Answering notes came from just behind her, and turning she found Gavin standing there giving an exact imitation of the bird.

'Gavin! You idiot! What on earth are

you doing here?'

'Looking for you.' He saw a flicker of alarm cross her face, so quickly reassured her: 'There's nothing wrong. I was just out for a stroll.'

He joined her on the bench, observing that there was another shower coming up the loch.

'How's the flat coming on?' he asked.

She groaned. 'It was in a bit of a mess and I seem to have spent hours scrubbing and polishing — but we're getting there.'

'I'd like to help,' he offered.

'You've helped enough, Gavin, moving and removing. I'm not going to let you do any more. But I do appreciate your kindness — oh, gosh! Here's that rain!'

Long spears of wet sleet came hurling at them from the west.

'It's going to be a downpour. Quick!' He leapt up, grabbed her arm, and ran with her to the nearest shelter, an overhang of rock, not far behind them, known as Creelers' Cave.

They were soon in the shelter, backs to the inner wall, looking out at the rainstorm.

'I want to help you,' Gavin said earnestly. 'I like you, Alison, as well as — I was going to say loving you, but I'd better say feeling attracted to you.'

She flushed with embarrassment but tried to cover it with a teasing remonstration.

'Gavin! You're incorrigible! It's not in order to be attracted to a married woman!'

He shook his head. 'You're no more married than I am. There was something wrong with that marriage of yours even before your husband went missing, wasn't there?'

As she made to protest he put his finger over her lips.

'D'you think I'd have said anything if I hadn't been aware of that?'

He put his arm round her shoulders, but she shrugged away, distressed, and took a pace away from him.

'Don't, Gavin.'

Loneliness could make you wistful. Arms empty for too long could make you vulnerable.

'Alison!' His expression was beguiling as he held out his arms to where she stood, huddled away from him. 'We're going to be here for a while,' he said, laughing. 'Come here till I give you a wee cuddle. You look so lonely and forlorn.'

She hated that description. She didn't want to seem the kind of woman men felt they had to care for.

She dragged in a deep breath, reaching down inside for the detachment she had schooled in herself, the control she had spent months mastering.

'Come here!' Gavin was insisting.

'No, Gavin! And if you don't stop teasing me I'll just run home in the rain.'

Putting action to words, she made for the opening but he pulled her back, his strong arms locking her against him.

'Don't!' She struggled, panicking.

'There, there!' he murmured as if speaking to a child. 'Let's start again where we left off when we were young . . . '

His lips were against her cold cheek, nuzzling round towards her mouth. He was warm, so warm — and comforting. It would be so easy . . .

Desperately she turned her head away from his seeking lips — and saw that the downpour was over. Surprising him with a quick movement, she was out of his arms, out of the cave and running back towards the village.

Disturbingly she could hear his voice, deep as the woods, as he shouted after her: 'You were the one! It was always you! Then you went away . . . '

Further Worries

Holding her mask in place and steadying her camera, Alison stepped from the boat into the water. The sense of freedom was heady.

Blithely she chased her own gleaming air bubbles back to the surface.

Breaking into the air again she gave the 'all's well' thumbs up signal to her back-up team and Sophy, standing with them on the deck, before duck-diving below once more.

Alison was down here to work. With the calm of the sheltered water and the sun shining above, visibility was superb. With smooth strokes, she guided herself down easily by the anchor rope.

It was a relatively shallow dive. Surely Keir McMaster could have no objection to her making it in his absence and on her own, although that was against the rules. She was anxious to get on with this part of her work.

She was a very experienced diver and had checked weather and tides — and, more importantly perhaps, consulted the skipper of the Kelpie.

He had anchored with perfect knowledge of where she wanted to dive, and had run up the blue and white diving flag.

The clarity of the water delighted her. She had to acknowledge that conditions looked good for the proposed oyster farm.

The camera was an encumbrance, but she wanted visual records for her own survey of the sea bed and its fauna. She took a good number of photographs as she studied the area, and then collected one or two specimens for examination back in the laboratory.

Satisfied with her survey, she turned and looked at the submerged rock-ledge that reached out into the water.

However, as she gazed, a strange eeriness touched her. A pair of black, gold-rimmed eyes were staring out at her from the darkness. The bullet-like head that contained them protruded from its deeply-curtained lair, moving in and out, in and out, snapping at invisible objects.

She watched as the head emerged still farther, then completely, to be followed by a seemingly never-ending, snake-like body. It was a conger eel, well over four feet long.

Her heart was pounding and her breathing laboured. The eel had startled her, and she felt foolishly shaken as she made for the surface.

The diving ladder was in place and willing hands took her cylinder and weight belt from her as she climbed on board. Hot coffee would be brewing up below.

As she stripped off her mask, Alison looked up to find herself confronted by Keir McMaster.

'I didn't receive your request for permission to dive,' he began, frowning, and then broke off as he looked into her face. 'Has something frightened you?'

'Where did you come from?' she asked inconsequentially.

He gestured impatiently to where one of the station's dinghies was tethered to the vessel.

She looked round anxiously for Sophy but she seemed to have gone below.

'Come on,' he said, 'let's get you down to a hot shower,' and he hustled her forward.

She hadn't thought of the research vessel having showers, but was glad to be guided to them and to begin the struggle to remove the tightly-adhering suit. She pulled the jacket up over the back of her head and brought it down outside-in in front, then found that her boss was tugging the sleeves off for her.

'I can manage,' she said stiffly, though she was frozen and exhausted.

He ignored her protest and peeled away the rest of her suit. She stepped out of it and stood in her black swimsuit, shivering violently.

He leaned across her to turn on the

shower in the cubicle behind her.

'Really, I can manage!' she exclaimed in exasperation — and stopped on a gasp at the strength of the charge that shot between them as he brushed against her.

She looked up into his face, confusion in her eyes. His hands were on her arms and suddenly his lips were on hers, hard and demanding. All his anger and anxiety for this headstrong woman were released in that kiss. His body felt taut against hers and a tiny moan rose in her throat as she responded to his touch.

An instant later, his head jerked back and as she regained her senses her eyes opened wide in realisation of what she was doing. With a violence born of self-disgust she pulled away.

Steam rose like smoke in the shower cubicle behind her. He leaned past her again to adjust the control, then propelled her under the stinging, reviving jets.

Keir avoided her eyes and his voice

was harsh when he spoke.

'I'll get the coffee,' he said above the noise of the water.

Alison was glad when he turned to leave her. She desperately wanted to be alone to make sense of her emotions. How could she be so affected by this man she hardly knew?

She had been shaken by that kiss and the feelings it had aroused ... How could she face him now?

When she was warm and dry and had dressed again, Alison made her way to the combined saloon-laboratory, where Keir was waiting with two steaming mugs of coffee.

His voice was so calm as he asked her about the dive that Alison wondered if she had imagined that swift, burning caress.

She took a deep breath, dragged her thoughts together and began to report on the dive and her findings.

'But what frightened you?' he asked after a while.

'Nothing. It was you. I wasn't

expecting you to be on the boat when I got back.'

He stared at her sceptically for so long that she had to admit: 'There's a good-sized conger eel down there if you want it for your collection.'

He grinned at her. 'Nine feet long?'

'No. More like four,' she said deflatingly.

'They can be savage. You have to be careful . . . '

'Yes, yes, of course.'

Keir was staring at her again.

'Why have you got your daughter on board?' he asked suddenly.

'Mainly because I thought you would never know,' Alison told him honestly. 'She's unhappy and not settling in at school,' she went on with difficulty. 'I've been trying to keep her amused during her holidays.'

'Take some days off.' His voice was unexpectedly gentle and understanding and her eyebrows shot up.

'I don't really need to,' she protested. 'I don't want to interrupt what I'm doing. If I could just bring her with me for a few days . . . ?'

'I don't want to give permission for that.' His face was inscrutable. 'Just imagine you never asked. If I don't see her or hear her — ' He shrugged. 'I didn't hear you ask, all right?'

The boat shuddered as it began to move through the water.

'Will that be all?' she asked as she gathered up the two mugs to take them back to the galley before looking for Sophy.

'No!' He barked out the word and she turned back, startled.

'Don't ever dive without my permission again,' he said incisively. 'And never alone.'

★ ★ ★

'I wonder, would you lend me a hand, Sophy? Could you bring your wheelbarrow over for a moment?' Sandy Matheson straightened up, putting a hand to the base of his spine and flexing wearily.

Sophy obligingly wheeled her barrow over the grass to the border.

'I'd as soon not bend down again to put the weeds in it. Would you do that for me, wee lass?'

'You're too old, Uncle Sandy,' Sophy scolded, bending and lifting small handfuls of weeds until they were all in the barrow.

'I'm not old at all, Sophy. I'm just a wee bit stiff, that's all. It happens to young lads like me now and again.' He smiled at her, thinking that it was good that she was chattering. She had been too quiet since starting school.

'And how are you enjoying all the jaunts your mother has been taking you on?' he asked.

'We went on a picnic today,' she announced.

'I know. Your friend Helen and her grandmother went with you. You didn't ask your old uncle to go too, though, did you?'

'Did you want to come? You could've

come, Uncle Sandy!' Sophy looked sorrowful that he had missed this treat.

'But where would you have taken me?' he asked.

'Away up a road among the trees.'

'I see — up one of the forest roads. And what did you find there, I wonder?'

'Helen's Uncle Gavin!' Sophy chortled. 'He came and he told us lots of things. And we played in the burn. Mum is friends with Gavin,' she reported.

Two women were approaching and as he recognised them, Sandy explained to his great-niece who they were.

'Here's the lady from the post office and her niece, Marie. Marie works at the marine station with your mum.

'Hello, Isa! Hello, Marie!' he called as they drew near.

Peggy, hearing her brother's greeting, came out of the house to meet their visitors.

'Hello, there — it's grand to see you. My, it's got much warmer — let's sit out here, shall we?'

She indicated the garden bench by the door, and while Isa McPhail sat down beside her, Marie left them and walked over to talk to Sandy and Sophy, her high heels sinking into the lawn with each step.

'Do you know Sophy, Marie?' Sandy asked.

'No, not yet. Hello, Sophy. I've met your mummy up at the station.'

Sophy smiled shyly at her. 'Hello.'

'You look smart today, lass,' Sandy commented, admiring Marie's red dress and shoes.

'Thanks, Sandy.' She glanced down at herself critically. 'I know my shoes don't *exactly* match this dress, but when I'm an actress, I'll have everything matching properly,' she vowed and smiled conspiratorially at Sophy, who was gazing up at her with something like hero-worship glowing in her eyes. Marie was the prettiest girl she had ever seen.

'Come over here, Marie, and do your own asking,' her aunt called out to her, and Marie turned to Sophy, holding out her hand.

'Come with me?' she appealed.

'All right.' Sophy felt important. This pretty girl wanted to be her friend.

Happily she took Marie's hand and Sandy watched them totter back across the grass with an amused smile playing about his lips.

Marie perched herself on the end of the bench and explained what it was that she wanted to ask.

'The Drama Club's having a coffee morning next Saturday to raise funds for going to the Festival. We're asking all our friends for help.'

'I see. And what would you be wanting me to do?' Peggy, true to form, was reluctant to commit herself.

Sandy had overheard and made his way over to join them.

'I'll put some cuttings in small pots,' he offered, 'and come over and sell them for you.'

Marie turned her dazzling smile on him.

'That would be terrific!' she enthused. 'We're having some stalls.'

'Would you like me to bake?' Peggy offered at last, determined not to be outdone.

'Would you?' Isa looked pleased. 'I've been telling Marie about your angel cakes. I'm so short of time to bake myself, I'm giving a donation instead — a good donation,' she added modestly.

'I'll do scones and pancakes and angel cakes for you, Marie. Will that help? Will you call for them on the morning?' Peggy asked, and Marie nodded.

'So are you back staying with your aunt now?' Peggy went on, knowing the girl had recently been staying in digs nearer to the marine station.

'No, she's not back with her aunt!' Isa said sharply. 'She only comes when she wants something.'

Seeing the cloud of mutiny descending on Marie's pretty features, Sandy stepped in swiftly.

'Come round to the greenhouse and I'll show you what I've got,' he suggested and took Sophy's hand, and the three had disappeared round the end of the house before Peggy could speak.

Isa turned to look despairingly at her friend, tears in her eyes.

'What will I do about Marie, Peggy? Her mother sent her here to help me care for Mother, but I never see her. And she's set her sights on becoming an actress, of all things!'

'Do nothing,' Peggy advised. 'She'll come round.'

'I sent for Mary — Marie's mother, you know — but, do you know, she says she can't come just now because they've got the decorators in! I ask you! Not a word that I'm the one who has Mother all the time. Not one of the others ever offers to take her for a week!'

Peggy was afraid that her friend was getting near the end of her tether.

'Now, Isa, you know it wouldn't do

for your mother to go away to a strange place,' she said gently. 'She'd be more confused than ever. And she's so happy with you.'

'Och, I know that, Peggy.' Isa took out a white, lace-edged hankie and wiped her eyes. 'I'm just being silly. I know she can't go anywhere else. It just comes over me at times. I'm just a stupid old woman.'

'You're not old, Isa,' Peggy scolded her. 'You and I are the same age!' She stood up. 'You're just overwrought. I'm going to get you a wee glass of sherry — that'll steady you.'

She went to the door and called into the house: 'Alison? Alison? Are you there, lass? Alison's making the supper,' she explained, turning back to Isa.

'Yes, Aunt Peggy?' Alison came hurrying out, clutching an oven cloth, her face flushed from the warmth of the kitchen.

'Would you mind bringing us out two glasses of sherry?'

'Of course. Coming up!'

Peggy was glad she'd thought of it when she saw how Isa seemed to relax a little with the sherry glass in her hand.

They were almost finished, and Isa was saying she'd left her mother long enough and must be going, when Sophy's cat Tabitha prowled over the grass with a mouse in her mouth.

As she laid her grisly trophy at Peggy's feet, Peggy's screams brought Alison running from the kitchen and the others from the back garden, and Isa forgot her troubles in her efforts to calm her friend. Meanwhile the terrified Tabitha streaked into the house and up the stairs to take refuge under the first duvet she came to.

She wasn't seen again all evening and everyone kind of forgot about her until Peggy, having enjoyed a good supper, decided on an early night and went upstairs to bed — only to find it was her bed Tabitha had taken refuge in! As Peggy climbed in, the cat shot out from under the duvet like a streak of lightning.

This time there was no consoling Peggy and she vowed that either the cat must go or she would be driven from her own home.

As Alison was changing the bedclothes at her aunt's insistence, Sophy, wakened by the din, came through to find her great-aunt huddled in a chair in a corner of the room and her mother spreading the freshly-covered duvet over the bed.

'It was Tabitha, Sophy,' Alison explained. 'She got into Aunt Peggy's bed. We'll take Tabitha and move into the flat right now, Aunt Peggy,' she went on soothingly. 'It's nearly ready. I'll just make up the beds for us . . .'

Peggy shook her head. 'Tomorrow will do, Alison. I don't think you should go tonight, and on a Sunday forby. Sandy wouldn't be pleased.'

'Tomorrow then,' Alison conceded. 'I'll get us flitted after work.

'Say goodnight to Aunt Peggy, Sophy. I can't tell you how sorry we are, Aunt Peggy. I'll bring you some aspirin and hot milk. And don't worry — we'll keep Tabitha out of your way, won't we, Sophy? She can stay outside meantime.'

★   ★   ★

The next morning, while her mother was getting ready for work, Sophy sneaked out and quietly deposited Tabitha on the back seat of the car and covered her with an anorak. Tabitha, after kneading her way round to make herself comfortable, nestled into the cocoon of the jacket and curled into a contented, loudly-purring ball, so that when Sophy's mother joined her, she found the child seated in the front passenger seat with her seat-belt fastened, singing 'Three Blind Mice' with surprising volume in an effort to drown out the purring.

Laughing, and relieved to see her daughter so happy for once, Alison joined in for a moment as she reached behind her to drop her carrier bag on the back seat.

'Right then! All ready to go? Have you got everything — crayons? Your colouring books? We're going to be working in the museum today — and I don't want you to go anywhere else. I've got biscuits and juice for you for morning break.' She put the car into gear. 'I'm going to be working in there with you, preparing an exhibit. We'll have fun!'

As it was the Easter holidays, quite a few visitors passed through the museum and the aquarium and Alison interrupted her work several times to talk to them.

Throughout, Sophy remained almost invisible, sitting on a stool at a little table in the corner, colouring her books.

Surely not even Keir McMaster could object to the little girl sitting there, Alison reasoned.

At half-past ten Alison went out to the car to get Sophy's picnic, but as she opened the car door, Tabitha saw her chance of freedom and shot past her and into the building.

'What — ?' Alison gasped. 'Tabitha!'

She realised at once what must have happened. No wonder Sophy had been singing so loudly!

'Tabitha! Tabitha! Come here!' Appalled, she set off in hot pursuit of the animal.

As Tabitha darted round the museum, Sophy had left her colouring and run after her, and had managed to track her down to a corner under a low table.

'Come on then, sweetie . . . ' Alison coaxed, and went down on her hands and knees to reach under the table — but just as she stretched out her hand to grab her, some visitors opened the door into the aquarium and Tabitha, seeing a way of escape, streaked past them and leapt, quivering, on to a bench beside a glass specimen tank.

'Oh no,' groaned Alison. 'If Keir McMaster sees this he'll go spare!'

Propelled by that thought she darted

after Tabitha and made a grab for her, but although she caught Tabitha firmly round her middle, the cat struggled and shot out her strong hind legs — and pushed the glass tank off the bench.

Alison watched in horror. It was as if it was happening in slow motion and there wasn't a thing she could do. Finally, with a dreadful splintering crash, the case hit the floor and glass, water and sea-life specimens splattered everywhere.

The commotion brought people running from every direction to see what all the noise was about, then it was all hands on deck to try to rescue the floundering specimens and clean up the mess.

In the furore she was vaguely aware of the cat making yet another escape and Sophy darting off after her, but the only conscious thought in her mind was to get this mess cleaned up quickly, before Keir McMaster saw it!

When, eventually, nothing remained to tell of the accident except the damp area on the floor of the aquarium, Sophy and Tabitha were nowhere to be seen and Alison headed off to try to find them.

However, as she went to leave the museum, she found her way barred by Keir McMaster.

'Can you tell me what's going on?' he asked.

'Excuse me,' she said, 'I've just got to find out where Sophy and Tabitha are before . . . '

'Sophy and Tabitha?'

'My daughter — and her cat,' she whispered, and saw his eyebrows shoot up in what was becoming a very familiar expression where he and she were concerned. Honestly, he must think she was nothing but trouble.

'And what are your daughter — and her cat — doing here?' he asked in a cool tone. 'I take it the noise I heard had something to do with them?'

'It was an accident. They never meant . . . Oh dear.' More people were coming along the passageway and she looked at him helplessly.

'Come this way.' He waved towards a door farther along the corridor and led the way into the general office where Marie was drinking her morning coffee.

As she looked up curiously, Keir made for an inner door that led to the office store-room.

'Come on — we can talk in here.'

'Oh, Keir,' Marie jumped up. 'Could you just glance at this? I can never find you! It won't take a moment.'

He stopped in mid-stride, bringing Alison to a sudden halt behind him, and took the papers Marie handed him.

As he glanced over them Marie lifted her coffee mug again then stepped towards him.

'There was one thing in particular I wanted you to check — ' she began, but then she appeared to stumble — and sent the contents of the mug cascading down the front of Alison's crisp white lab coat.

As Alison jerked back, startled, Keir swung round.

'For goodness sake! Are you all right?'

Alison turned to him but found his eyes were on Marie, whose face was a picture of wide-eyed dismay.

'Yes,' she breathed. 'I just seemed to — trip somehow. I'm so sorry! Silly shoes.'

'Well, no real harm done,' he observed. 'This is perfect, Marie!' He finished looking over the papers and handed them back. 'Excellent.'

Marie drank in his words, innocent violet eyes raised to his in admiration.

'Oh, thank you, Keir,' she murmured. 'I love working for you.'

He turned to Alison. 'In here!' he commanded, his voice harsh as he held the store-room door open for her.

The small room was used as a stationery store.

'Now,' he said, turning to her, 'tell me what's going on. And you'd better take that off, too,' he added, indicating the lab coat with its coffee stain.

Slowly she began to undo the

buttons, reluctant to shed the equalising uniform, feeling, somehow, that she was being divested of her armour.

When she had removed it, she felt absurdly naked as he regarded her, and to avoid that critical appraisal she turned her back to him and gazed out of the window that looked out on the land to the back of the station.

Over the wall and up a steep bank, a sloping field was crowned by a wood of tightly-planted pines. Beyond the forest, huge granite boulders rested and then the mountain — the nearest to the sea of the range — rose up behind Torquillan.

'Now, tell me — ' he began, 'what were your daughter — and her cat — doing here?'

She shrugged. 'I told you about Sophy.'

'That's true. But I thought you understood my position. I thought you would be subtle enough . . . ' His eyes gleamed with anger. 'And the cat?'

'The cat.' Alison shook her head and

put her hand to her brow in a gesture of defeat. 'My Aunt Peggy has an aversion to cats and . . . well, I think Sophy must have been trying to protect Tabitha and, unknown to me, smuggled her into the car. When I went out for our picnic and opened the door she escaped and ran into the building with . . .'

'With disastrous consequences!' he finished for her.

'Yes,' she whispered. 'You know the rest?'

'I'm afraid so,' he agreed wearily. 'Look, I'm responsible for this station. I have to see that it runs smoothly and efficiently — the public part as well as the research for the moment. I can't allow the place to be disrupted or given a bad name.'

She glanced surreptitiously at her watch. It was almost an hour since she'd last seen Sophy, and she prayed that this interview might soon be over.

'I know,' she said placatingly, 'and I'm sorry. It won't happen again,' she promised. 'I'll ask Mrs Dunbar to have

Sophy from tomorrow — and we'll shut the cat in the flat.'

He nodded, but kept staring at her as though he found it difficult to look away.

'You've no idea,' she suddenly burst out, 'what it's like to have a child to worry about. You've only yourself!'

'Ah, but I do know.' He spoke so softly that she barely heard him. 'I once had a baby son.'

'Once?' She looked up in startled contrition. 'Oh! I'm sorry!'

His face had gone grey and he gave a stiff shrug.

'You didn't know.'

'You're married?' she asked tentatively.

'Has the local grapevine omitted to tell you?' He spoke wearily. 'Anyway, I'm not married any longer.'

She wanted to find out more, but before she could speak he came at her with another question.

'This is hardly a satisfactory situation. Where is — er, Sophy's father?'

It seemed the local grapevine had failed to keep him informed, too, she thought.

'He was working for an oil company in the Middle East,' she explained. 'He went on a Kenyan safari and disappeared. He hasn't been seen since.'

'I see. How long ago?'

'A year,' she told him calmly.

He studied her as though searching for her true feelings and she tried to keep her expression blank.

'May I go now?' she asked with feigned humility.

'Yes. But — ' He waved a hand towards her. ' — tidy up your life, please. Remember, this is neither a nursery nor a circus.'

She ignored the jibe, taking a last look towards the hills, feeling sick with a sudden vague premonition that that was the way Sophy had gone. The corridor from the museum ran straight to the back of the building. What if the rear door had been open? It would have led them straight out there.

Sophy's Lost!

Alison spent the whole of her lunch hour looking for them. First she drove home, but neither Sandy nor Peggy had seen any sign of them. She went to ask Bess Dunbar and Helen, but they couldn't help either. Nor had any of the shopkeepers seen them pass, and no-one had seen them on the shore.

The consensus of opinion was that the cat must have run up the hill, and that Sophy had pursued her.

'Sophy'll never find her,' Aunt Peggy predicted gloomily. 'Cats panic in new places and get lost.'

'Maybe — but I've got to find Sophy.' Keeping her expression calm, Alison fought to keep down the rising panic in her breast and headed back to the marine station.

Parking her car behind the station, she grabbed Sophy's anorak from the back seat and started up the brae, trying to remember what her daughter had been wearing. As she walked she was aware that she was mentally preparing the description that she would have to give the police if she couldn't find her.

With no path through them, the pines were closely planted and made a dark, frightening forest where little else could grow. Alison shivered, trying to imagine how her little girl would feel scrambling over the rutted ground in this dim light.

'Sophy! Sophy!' she began to shout, her stomach churning with fear.

In the distance she could see brighter light — was that the end of the wood?

'Sophy! Sophy! Answer me, Sophy! Oh, Sophy — don't be lost! I can't bear it! Darling, where are you?' she pleaded, her heart hammering in her breast. 'Sophy! Sophy!'

If I could just get out of this terrible wood, she thought. Once I'm above it, perhaps I'll be able to see the whole hillside.

Don't think about the pools among the rocks, she told herself. Don't think about the bogs. She'll be all right — she has to be!

'Sophy! Sophy!' She felt panic rising inside her as she continued towards the light.

When she finally stumbled out of the wood, her voice was hoarse from calling and her breath was rasping in her throat. But suddenly — was that a faint cry, coming from somewhere far to her right?

She held her breath. Had it been a human cry or only the scream of a gull?

She turned and began to climb again in the direction of the sound.

The climb had been steep from the station and she had been practically running, and she had to stop for a moment to ease the agony in her legs and chest.

As she fought for breath she looked around. She could see a farmhouse over on the village side of the wood.

We'll go there on our way down, she told herself, determinedly optimistic. When I've found Sophy — not if, but when! — we'll call in there — and I'll phone to let Keir know where I am.

'Sophy! Sophy!' Her voice carried clearly across the mountain and an unexpected answering shout caused her pulse to leap.

She looked around, her heart thudding, and saw a group of people coming down the mountainside. Gavin was leading them, a young woman by his side.

It must be a group returning from one of the guided walks that the Forestry Commission ran, she realised. Although forest management was Gavin's main concern, his job also included leading tourist walks during holiday periods, she knew.

'Have you seen Sophy?' she shouted long before they reached her. 'She's lost!'

'Hold on!' Gavin hurried towards

her, the others hastening after him.

When Alison had explained what had happened, they all spread out over the hillside, without losing sight of each other, as Gavin had instructed, and began a sweep search of the whole area.

Suddenly Gavin heard a cry and held up his hand to attract the attention of the others. Everyone halted to listen — and the sound came again.

'That must be her!' he said. 'Sophy! We're coming!' Gavin shouted encouragingly. 'Where are you, lass?'

Then they all heard it — a whimpering cry from somewhere below. They made for a formation of boulders over to the left.

The rocks were strewn haphazardly, some firmly embedded in the soil, others precariously balanced. Between the stones were thin tracks of straw-coloured grass, bleached by the snow and ice of the winter and slippery as chutes.

Beneath the rocks a steep cliff

plunged away to the water. Seagulls wheeled above, their raucous calls splintering the air.

While in pursuit of Tabitha, Sophy had lost her footing and had slipped down the slope until one of the great stones had halted her. Too frightened to move, she was crouched against the rock, crying quietly.

Tears of relief almost blinded Alison.

'Darling, don't worry! It's Mummy! I'm here!' Her voice was jerky with emotion.

An experienced climber and wearing hiking boots as he was, Gavin managed the scramble down to rescue Sophy without much difficulty. Carefully he enveloped her in his arms and brought her back up to solid ground, and when he set her down she ran straight into her mother's open arms.

'Thank God you're safe,' Alison whispered, hugging her tightly and battling to control her emotions. She took a deep breath then turned to the walking party.

'What can I say? Thank you so much!'

The child seemed frozen stiff and Gavin urged them to hurry down the hill. But Sophy kept turning round and trying to go back as they encouraged her to descend.

'Where's Tabitha?' she kept asking in distress. 'I want Tabitha!'

'I don't know where she is, darling. I'm sorry.' Alison had to keep a tight hold of her hand as she wriggled to free herself.

'You can't go after her any more,' Gavin pronounced sternly, lifting the child into his arms. 'She'll be hiding somewhere and we'd never find her now. I'll look out for her when I'm on the hills, but right now we have to get you home. You're shivering and we have to get you warm again. All right?'

His stern tone seemed to do the trick and at last she stopped struggling.

'I must go into the first house we come to and phone Keir McMaster,'

Alison told him. 'I ran off in search of Sophy without saying where I was going. Oh, here's the farmhouse I saw — and here's the gate! I'll pop in here.'

'It's not a farmhouse now — ' Gavin began, lowering Sophy to the path once more, but Alison interrupted.

'You'd better go on. Your party will be overdue and they'll be sending out a search party for you as well! We'll be fine now.'

He hesitated and glanced at his watch. 'You're right — I should get them back. We are overdue — we were supposed to be back for lunch.' He grinned ruefully. 'I'll have to go with them. Are you sure you'll be all right? Mrs Craig will let you use the phone here. And ask her to give Sophy a hot drink.'

'I will. And thanks, Gavin.'

'I'll check round later.' He waved as he went striding off with the walking party.

Sophy was shivering violently as

Alison pressed the bell beside the handsome wooden door. The farmhouse appeared to have been lovingly restored.

'Are you very cold, darling?' she asked in concern but Sophy's teeth were chattering so much that she couldn't answer.

'Oh, my goodness! What's happened?' The lady who opened the door looked in dismay at the ashen-faced, shivering child and the pale woman. 'Come in. Come into the kitchen and get warm.' She held the door wide. 'I'll get you some hot drinks.'

'I'm sorry to disturb you but could I use your phone?' Alison asked.

'Of course.' The woman waved towards the telephone in the living room then reached out to take Sophy's hand.

'Come with me, wee girl,' she said kindly and led her to a seat beside the stove in the kitchen.

As she picked up the receiver and dialled, Alison noticed with some surprise that her fingers were trembling.

It was Marie who answered her call.

'Marie, it's Alison Evans. Can I speak to Dr McMaster, please?'

'Oh, so it's you, is it?' Marie sounded pert. 'He's been looking for you everywhere!' There was something about her tone that disturbed Alison.

Keir was soon on the line.

'Where are you now?' he demanded when she had explained what had happened.

'Just a minute . . . What's the name of your house?' she called to the lady in the kitchen.

'Springhill,' came the reply.

Alison relayed the name to Keir. 'We're at a house called Springhill.'

After a short pause a dry laugh echoed back to her.

'I see. Just wait there.' There was amusement as well as weariness in his voice. 'Let the child rest and have a hot bath and food.'

'But I can't ask for . . . ' she began to protest but he quickly interrupted.

'Yes you can. Let me speak to Mrs Craig, please.'

'Yes. All right. Mrs Craig! Could you come to the phone, please?'

Mrs Craig appeared in the doorway. 'Who is it?'

'It's my boss, Dr McMaster.'

'Mine too!' the woman whispered conspiratorially as she took the receiver, leaving Alison looking at her askance.

Did she mean — oh, please, no! — this couldn't possibly be Keir McMaster's house!

★　★　★

She quizzed Mrs Craig the moment she came back, and so it proved. This was Keir McMaster's home and Mrs Craig was his daily help.

Alison felt a thrill of dismay and would have walked out at that very moment had it not been for Sophy. The child needed immediate care and Mrs Craig was already running a bath for her.

Warmed by the bath and a bowl of hot broth, Sophy was put to bed in a spare room and was soon sound asleep, leaving Alison free to join Mrs Craig for a cup of coffee in the lounge.

She tried to convey her gratitude for all she had done for them.

Blushing, the woman brushed off her thanks. 'Och, away with you — I was just following doctor's orders!' She laughed. 'But what about you? You need a rest, too. Won't you have forty winks?'

'Oh, no! Thank you, but I couldn't.' Not in Keir McMaster's home. 'I'd just like to stay here, if you don't mind, till Sophy wakes. It's a lovely room,' she commented.

Tastefully furnished, each fine piece blended perfectly with the character of the old house.

'And an incredible view!' she went on, looking to the three big windows which faced out over the hill. 'So much sky — and the loch 'way below!'

'Isn't it? It's because we're so high up. Now, if you'll excuse me, I must get on — I've a casserole to prepare for supper.' She glanced up as she gathered up their coffee cups. 'You're sure you don't want to lie down for a while?'

'Thank you, but no. And I'm sorry we've kept you back.'

'Not at all. I've enjoyed your company.' She smiled. 'Is there anyone else you need to contact? Please feel free to use the phone.'

'Well, if I could just give my Uncle Sandy a quick call — ?'

Mrs Craig nodded and prepared to leave.

'You do that then have a wee rest,' she said kindly. 'I'll come back with some tea later on.'

'Thank you — it's very kind of you.'

Alison phoned her uncle to explain what had happened, and assured him that they were both fine now, then paced around the room restlessly for a few minutes before pausing by the bookshelves flanking the fireplace.

Selecting a novel that caught her eye, she sank into a comfortable armchair, and just managed to read the back cover before her eyelids drooped and her eyes softly closed . . .

She slept deeply for some time and then she experienced a dreadful dream. She dreamed of Clive in the African bush — that he had been captured by a fierce tribe . . .

★   ★   ★

Keir McMaster arrived home quite a bit before his usual time. 'Goodness, you're early,' Mrs Craig remarked, rising from the kitchen table where she had been sitting with Sophy, and going to switch on the kettle.

'Yes. I thought I'd better come and see how things were here. Hello, Sophy.' He took a seat across the table from the girl and studied her. 'How are you now?'

'Fine, thank you,' came the polite reply.

'She's had a lovely sleep and she's looking much better, aren't you, love?'

Mrs Craig was taking china out of a cupboard and setting a tray. 'She's upset about losing her cat, mind. But she's a very brave girl, aren't you, pet? Just you drink up your cocoa. You'll soon forget about it, I'm sure.'

Keir doubted that but said nothing.

He watched as the child obediently lifted her mug and drank from it and then began to push pieces of bread about her plate, forming them into a square.

Suddenly she sensed his scrutiny and sent him a roguish smile, and he found himself quite affected by it. There was something about her — something he preferred to resist — tugging at his heart strings.

'I'm sure we can find a little kitten for you,' he commented. 'In fact, there are going to be some here quite soon. Would you like one?'

'A kitten?' Sophy's green eyes sparkled with interest but then, just as suddenly, the light went out of them. 'No, thank you,' she told him in a very grown-up manner. 'Great-Aunt Peggy doesn't want a cat near and it would be difficult for Mummy.'

'Oh, I see. Well . . . ' Poor kid, he was thinking, and he tried to imagine how she was feeling. First her father's disappearance — and then being brought to this completely foreign environment full of strangers . . . It must all be deeply disturbing for her. 'Well, we'll have to think of something else,' he finished lamely, feeling a strange urge to gather the child up in his arms and shield her from all that troubled her.

'Where's her mother?' he asked the housekeeper, looking around.

'Sound asleep, in the lounge. I looked in with a cup of tea but decided to leave her. Poor girl — she's worn out.' She put the finishing touches to the tea tray. 'But I'll just take this through now and waken her.'

He stood up. 'I'll take it. I have to have a word with her anyway.'

He saw her as soon as he walked into

the room, slumped in his armchair, still deep in sleep. About to speak and wake her, he paused, unable to stop staring at her.

The normally sparkling eyes were hidden by almost transparent lids. Shadows touched the ivory cheeks. She looked, in sleep, almost too tired to breathe. But her hands were gripping convulsively and a dreadful moan escaped her lips.

'Alison,' he said quietly, then again, slightly louder — 'Alison!'

Her eyes flew open as she woke from her nightmare.

'What on earth's the matter?' he asked. 'Are you ill? You were moaning as though you were in anguish.'

'Mental anguish,' she said faintly, putting her hand to her brow and rubbing it in an effort to clear her brain. 'The most appalling nightmare . . .'

Suddenly she remembered where she was and pulled herself upright.

'Is Sophy all right?' she asked urgently.

'Perfectly. She's in the kitchen with Mrs Craig.'

'Thank God!' Flustered, she struggled to her feet causing the book to fall from her lap onto the floor. 'Oh, I hope you don't mind — I was looking for something to keep myself occupied while Sophy rested. I didn't mean to sleep myself. I must go . . . '

'Sit down,' he ordered. 'I've brought you some tea.'

'No! Thank you,' she replied stiffly. 'We've presumed on your hospitality too long.'

'Don't be silly.' He placed a cup of tea on a table beside her, then fixed her with a stern gaze. 'You really must try to take better care of your child,' he said abruptly.

The blood rushed to her cheeks and she felt her temples pounding. The continuing arrogance of this man amazed her.

'My God!' she yelled at him. 'Who do you think you are? And what do you think I'm trying to do? And anyway, if it hadn't been for you, keeping me back when I wanted to go after her this morning, none of this would have happened!'

'May I remind you that Sophy shouldn't have been at the station in the first place.' His eyes were cold. 'And a marine station, as I mentioned before, is hardly the place for a cat!'

'I've already apologised for that.'

'Agreed. But look, I'm thinking of the child. What if something had happened to her?'

'I don't believe this!' She ran her hand through her hair. 'She is my whole concern! While trying to do my work, I'm also attempting to be the best mother, father, provider, companion, cook, housekeeper, nursemaid in the world! She's unhappy at school — and now to cap it all the cat's gone. And she loved Tabitha!'

To her dismay, her vehemence seemed to cause a wave of faintness to wash over her. She was furious with herself for her weakness but soon the colour had ebbed from her face.

'I'll work an extra half-day in lieu of this afternoon,' she ground out, trying to control the swaying of her body.

He caught her as she crumpled and, for a moment, she was pressed against his chest, aware of the thudding of his heart before she was gently lowered on to the chair.

She knew nothing more until she heard Mrs Craig's voice.

'Have you eaten anything since morning?' she asked gently.

'Mmm — no, I just had coffee, I think,' Alison admitted.

'I'll fetch her something,' Mrs Craig told Keir and hurried away.

They both stood over Alison as she ate the scrambled eggs and toast Mrs Craig brought, and they certainly made her feel stronger.

Nevertheless she stumbled as she stood up too quickly and a strong hand immediately grasped her elbow. Her breathing quickened at Keir's touch but his face was inscrutable.

Brushing aside her protestations that she would get a taxi, Keir insisted on driving them home.

Alison was glad when he left them at the door and didn't come in — everything about him was too unsettling for her to cope with right now.

However she stood and watched the big black car slip smoothly down the drive and take the road back through the village again before she turned and opened the door.

A Shock In Store

When the Torquillan club won the District Amateur Drama Festival, everyone threw themselves into preparations for the divisional finals in Inverness.

Marie was walking on air after the local triumph, delighted by the praise her acting had received, while Gavin, the club's leading man, was uncharacteristically nervous on the last night of the finals and had persuaded Alison to come along for moral support.

She soon got involved in helping out with the stage make-up.

'Don't make me too beautiful,' Gavin begged as she carefully smoothed make-up over his face and neck. 'Aren't you glad I made you come though?'

'It's good fun — but I'm scared I'll get this wrong and you'll look like Frankenstein's monster!' she admitted. 'It was good of your mum to look after

Sophy, wasn't it?'

'Och, she was glad to — especially since she had Helen anyway. She says it's easier to have them both.'

'Right, shut up and keep still now — I want to paint your lips.'

'Yeuch! I don't know how you women can be bothered going through this palaver every day!'

'Shush!' Alison giggled. 'You know, I don't know when I've enjoyed myself so much.'

Although their performance seemed to go well, when the summing up was done at the end of the evening, it emerged that Torquillan had not won the final. However, Marie once again had been singled out for special acclaim and was awarded the trophy for the best individual performance.

One of the most interesting aspects of the competition for each drama group was the private adjudication process, where constructive advice — and criticism — was given by the adjudicators and received with varying degrees of enthusiasm by the players.

When it was Torquillan's turn, the chief adjudicator, Roger Ellis, perched on the table in the little side room where they had assembled and enjoyed a good argument with them about the merits and demerits of the play they had chosen.

He knew what he was talking about. After many years of treading the boards, he told them, he now held a lectureship at one of the colleges of dramatic art.

When the cast were leaving he called Marie back to talk to her privately.

'I wanted to congratulate you on an outstanding performance — by any standards.'

She flushed with pride. 'Oh! Thank you!'

'What are you doing away up here in the north?' he went on. 'You're gifted. Are you going to hide yourself here for ever? Don't you mean to study, to improve?' he demanded, and Marie gasped, her eyes growing wide at his vehemence. 'Is there a reason? A boyfriend?' he persisted.

'Well . . . ' She paused and shrugged helplessly. 'My mother sent me up here to help my aunt who . . . needed some support.'

'Sent you up from where?' he pressed.

'Glasgow.'

'Glasgow!' He echoed incredulously, and his expressive mouth widened in a smile. 'Where you have the splendid Royal Scottish Academy of Dramatic Art on your doorstep! But . . . ' He looked at her keenly. ' . . . you've met someone here, I suppose? You don't want to go back?'

Her cheeks flushed. 'There is a man I'm attracted to,' she admitted.

He nodded, then fixed her with a stern look.

'And if I were to ask you what you want most in the world, what would you tell me?'

'To be an actress . . . ' she said at once.

'Well, then — '

'But you don't understand,' she interrupted him, tears gathering in her eyes. 'I've only ever wanted to be an actress. But in our house it — well, it just isn't what you do. So I was persuaded to do secretarial studies instead. And now it's too late, isn't it? How could I go to drama college now?'

He put his hands on her shoulders and looked her straight in the eye.

'It's never too late to follow your star. There would be auditions, of course. You might even qualify for a grant.' He studied her for a long moment more. 'Look,' he said suddenly, 'perhaps I could help prepare you for an audition.' He took a card out of his wallet and handed it to her, adding, 'but you'd have to make up your mind quickly. What d'you think?'

'I don't know!' she squealed, her heart leaping with excitement. 'I don't know! I can't think.'

'Well, when you've calmed down a bit, do think — then let me know. Now,

117

we'd better see about joining the others.'

And he took her elbow and led her out to join some of the others who were waiting to escort him to the party they had organised in their hotel.

★ ★ ★

The party was being held in the main lounge of the hotel and the few tourists who were there were quickly included in the fun.

Marie had persuaded Keir McMaster to be one of the chauffeurs for the expedition and was doing her best to charm him.

Alison's car had also been pressed into use. Some of the costumes had been transported in the back, and Gavin had chosen to be her passenger in preference to taking his pick-up.

Gavin was determined that Alison should have a good time and forget all her worries for a while but she found it difficult to relax. Every time she raised her eyes it seemed to be Keir McMaster who met her gaze, and soon he and Marie joined them.

'I hope we're not intruding,' Marie apologised coyly.

'Not at all. There's nothing to intrude on — yet,' Gavin teased. 'Though we were childhood sweethearts so who can say what might happen?' and to Alison's absolute embarrassment he lifted her hand to his lips and kissed it.

She parried Gavin's nonsense as best she could, embarrassingly aware of her boss's appraising, sidelong glances.

I hope he doesn't think I'm encouraging Gavin, she despaired. Gavin was a well-known flirt and she was sure he was just showing off to Marie that he wasn't heartbroken because she'd lost interest in him. It was Marie he really wanted, she was sure.

'Alison, what would you like to drink?' Gavin asked. 'Everyone else has got one.'

'Don't trouble yourself, Gavin — I'll

just go and see what they have.'

She shot up and went to the bar before anyone could stop her.

As she stood waiting for the barman, she was joined by one of the hotel guests who touched her arm gently.

'It's Mrs Evans, isn't it? Mrs Alison Evans?'

Alison looked at the young man in surprise.

'Yes . . . '

'I thought it was. I've seen your photograph — Clive showed it to me.'

She felt the blood drain from her face.

'Clive? You've seen Clive?'

'I was with him in Saudi. I'm an oil engineer, too, you see.' He paused for a moment. 'I had heard you were at Torquillan. I was going to get in touch. I was on that safari with him — '

Alison reached a hand out to the bar to steady herself.

'So — so you know where he is?' she whispered.

'I'm sorry to do this when you

seemed so . . . happy. But yes, I think I do.'

★   ★   ★

When a Dashing White Sergeant was announced almost everyone took to the floor. Only Keir McMaster and Roger Ellis remained seated at a corner table.

The noise of the music and merriment was deafening.

'Let's go where we can talk,' Alison's companion suggested, pointing to a small sitting-room across the entrance hall.

She stole a glance at her boss in the mirror behind the bar and observed him giving her a long curious glance as she turned away and let the engineer escort her out of the room.

She set her glass down on a coffee table in the little sitting-room, then lowered herself into a chair. There was a dull weight inside her and she felt physically sick.

Jim Muir was a Scot with the gift of

tale spinning. He wanted to tell Alison all about the safari just before Clive had disappeared, and was at pains to draw an accurate picture for her of all that had happened on that fateful holiday.

'We flew from Bahrain to Nairobi, then we took a smaller plane to the game reserve.' His words scraped along her nerves and she longed to tell him to stop. 'When we landed we were met by a Range-Rover and taken to a safari lodge — but we'd decided that we wanted to go to a bush camp away from the tourist route so we drove another thirty miles across the bush to this camp by a river. We were under canvas, of course; Clive and I shared a tent.

'Well, we enjoyed several days of safari then Clive started to be very — disagreeable.'

Alison stared at him. 'What do you mean? What happened?'

'Oh, he began to complain a lot, which was daft because if you want the Ritz you go to the safari lodges. But we'd plumped for camping! Then he started arguing with the safari guides — as if they didn't know best, with all their experience.

'They warned us never to go out into the bush alone, but everybody knows that. We even had a big Masai on guard outside all night. I don't know how Clive got out without me wakening or the Masai seeing him. He must have been pretty stealthy.

'I guess he must have been miffed with some of the organisers, but anyway, perhaps just before dawn, he slipped out. Maybe he wanted to prove something. He took his camera with him — to get some shots of a leopard we'd seen, I reckon.'

'So what happened to him?' she pressed but Jim shrugged.

'Well, when we discovered that he'd gone — and then he didn't come back — a big search was organised, but they found no trace of him. However, they did discover that a band of ivory poachers had killed an elephant not far away — and this brings me to my theory.

'If Clive disturbed them ... well, they're pretty ruthless characters but there was no sign of — of a body,' he said quickly, and saw her flinch. 'So it's possible that they took him prisoner and hauled him away out of the area that was searched.

'One of the game patrols arrested a big gang of poachers just before I left Bahrain so maybe we'll have more definite news soon.'

He paused and reached out to touch her hand.

'I'm sorry, Alison, but I have to say that I don't think there's much hope of finding him alive now.'

Alison nodded, surprised at how calm she felt.

Jim Muir stood up. 'I'm going to get you some brandy. You look awfully pale.'

'I'm all right,' Alison faltered. 'I suppose I already knew most of what you've told me. It's just that — you've brought it all so vividly to life.'

She looked up at him, at his kind, anxious expression.

'It must have been awful for you, too,' she acknowledged.

'Pretty rough,' he agreed. 'Reports — interrogations — ' He gave her a bleak smile. 'I don't like thinking about it. But I always promised myself I'd contact you when I got home. I went to your Colchester address, and they told me I'd find you here.'

'Well, thank you . . . ' Alison managed a thin smile. 'It was kind of you to come.'

* * *

Alison couldn't sleep. She seemed to have been in bed for hours and so far the hotel hadn't settled down for the night. Footsteps echoed down the corridor, doors opened and closed, light still streamed through the transom.

Her mind was in a turmoil, thoughts of Clive crowding in on her.

Their wedding had been the happiest day of her life. But, she now realised, she hadn't really known Clive's true personality then. Charming and spontaneous, he had also been prone to sudden changes of mood with a quick temper. Soon — too soon — there had been constant rows, besides which she had had to adjust to his long absences from home on business. One of Alison's friends had even hinted that he'd found someone else.

It had been a long time since there had been any real love between them. It had been Sophy who had kept them together.

Alison sighed deeply. She'd begun to believe that Jim's guess could be correct — that Clive had been taken by poachers. If only she knew what had really happened. Would she ever know?

If no trace of him was found, he couldn't be declared dead for seven years. Would she have to spend those years linked to a man who could nevertheless be dead?

Restlessly she threw off the bed-clothes. She needed some air. It was two in the morning, but she didn't care. She dressed and left her room to go for a walk. The hotel opened on to the town's main street which was well lit, she recalled. She would just take a quick stroll round the block to clear her head.

When she reached the downstairs hall, she saw Jim Muir playing cards with three other men in a corner of the lounge.

Keir McMaster was coming in through the entrance and approaching the desk, but he paused when he caught sight of her.

'If you're looking for your oil-man he's playing cards,' was his greeting.

'I'm not looking for anyone!' she returned quickly, and her eyes widened with anger at his implication. How dare he? 'I'm going for a walk!' she snapped.

'Not alone.' He swung round from the desk. 'You can't go out walking alone at this hour.'

'Of course I can!' She shot defiantly through the swing door, unaware that he was just behind her.

She heard a car approaching but the traffic lights at the junction at the corner were at red, she noticed, and she heard the gears changed. As it slowed she stepped on to the road and began to hurry across — just as the car accelerated again. The lights were still red but the driver must have decided, since it was the middle of the night, that there was no need to obey them.

Suddenly an arm encircled her waist and she was lifted bodily backwards as the car raced past, almost grazing her.

It had been such a narrow shave that she thought for a moment she had been hit. She leaned against the wall of the hotel porch, her heart racing.

Keir, her rescuer, was beside her, his arm curved protectively on the wall above her head, and she leaned against him, grateful for his strength.

He was holding her now, his lips descending to touch hers, comforting and gentle, and she felt the tension leave her body as she relaxed against him, losing herself in his kiss.

Then suddenly she pushed him away, anger and guilt washing over her. How dare he take advantage of her moment of weakness!

'Thank you for rescuing me,' she said a little unsteadily. 'I don't think I'll go for a walk now,' she went on, moving away. 'It was very hot. I couldn't sleep, but now . . . '

'I'm sure Gavin would have escorted you if he'd known you wanted to walk,' he observed.

'I'm sure he would,' she answered with spirit.

'Or the oil-man . . . ' he persisted.

She walked ahead of him through the reception area towards the stairs, saying over her shoulder. 'For your information, the oil-man brought me news of my husband.' And she began to climb the stairs without looking back.

As he watched her begin to make her weary way up to her room, he saw her shoulders droop. She looked, he thought, as though she had the worries of the world on those shoulders.

* * *

'The child is stressed,' the educational psychologist stated, looking earnestly at Alison through outsize spectacles.

She was very young and wore no rings. Unmarried, Alison thought, and presumably had never brought up a child herself. Probably very clever, though, and with all sorts of degrees and experience.

'It's not uncommon,' the expert continued. 'New school, new friends to make, a strange environment, not knowing Gaelic when all her schoolmates do — and with an English accent to make it even more difficult. Some of the other children were teasing her, I'm afraid. The physical sickness was a manifestation of nervous anxiety. However, the teacher has spoken to the class now, so we're hoping the teasing will die down. What we have to do now is build up Sophy's confidence and sense of security.'

Alison gave a weary sigh. 'I do try but it's such a juggling act all the time. You've got to keep your end up at work — and then you come home and you want to give your child all your attention but you're exhausted.' She pushed her hand distractedly through her hair. 'You just have no energy left.'

'Yes, I know,' the woman agreed with genuine sympathy. It was a story she heard so often these days. 'Sophy's very intelligent, though. More than that, she's an unusually sensitive child, and she senses your fatigue — and your problems. That's why she didn't want to trouble you about the teasing.'

'Poor love!' Alison put her hands over her eyes for a moment and shook her head. 'But I'm not a worse parent because I'm alone at present.' She felt her voice rising in protest. 'Sophy's father was abroad most of the time anyway. I know you're thinking that because there's only me, she doesn't get the time and consideration she needs. But it's just not true. I work twice as hard to be a good parent — but I have to have a job to support us!'

'You're getting upset, Mrs Evans . . . '

'Don't patronise me, please,' Alison retorted, and the woman held out her hands in appeal.

'I'm sorry, that's not what I'm trying to do — I do understand how difficult it must be for you. Are there any other adults Sophy is close to?'

'There's my uncle. My Uncle Sandy and Sophy are great friends.'

'Good. Let's encourage that — give Sophy another anchor, as it were.'

'You may be sure that I'll continue doing all I can,' Alison returned and the other woman nodded.

'Well, I'll see Sophy again in a month and see how things are then. I'm sure she's just needing time to settle in.'

Alison pushed her chair back and rose to her feet, thankful the meeting was over.

'Can I come in, Aunt Isa?' Marie Blair stood on Isa's doorstep, a suitcase in each hand.

Isa looked up then turned to her mother, rocking in her chair by the fire.

'Look, Mother — look what the tide's brought in — bags and all! It looks as though you're back,' she commented, turning back to the girl.

'My room was let to summer visitors,' Marie explained.

'Well, I'm glad you're back, lass,' Isa admitted. 'It was quiet without you.'

'Is this the nurse then?' old Agnes McPhail asked, peering towards Marie.

'No, it's your granddaughter, Marie,' Isa explained patiently. 'You remember Marie?'

'Hi, Gran!' Marie moved to kiss the old woman's cheek, then glanced up at Isa. 'I won't be staying long, mind,' she told her. 'I'm going down to Glasgow to do auditions for drama college soon.'

'Oh, I see. And will you be staying in Glasgow long?' Isa was curious to know.

'Only for a fortnight — I've got two weeks' leave. I'll be coming back after that. I want to be here for the drama club summer season.'

'And after that?'

'I don't know. It depends. Even if I pass the auditions and get a place at college, I don't know if I'll accept it. But I should know by September what I want to do.'

'When are you leaving?'

'Tomorrow morning. Keir McMaster's driving down for a conference and he's giving me a lift. It was too good a chance to miss.'

'Oh, I'm sure.' Isa smiled. 'And how's Alison Evans getting on?'

'Alison? Oh, Keir's told her she's to spend the summer in a caravan on the wrong side of the loch, monitoring an experiment.'

Isa looked askance. 'But what about Sophy?'

Marie shrugged. 'She'll be with her, I suppose.'

'And you're away tomorrow with Dr McMaster? And here's me thinking I was going to get some help with your gran.'

'But I'm no bother to you, Isa!' Agnes protested.

'No, Mother.' Isa managed a smile. 'Of course you aren't.'

★　★　★

Sandy Matheson sat on a wooden bench, looking out over the bay. He was waiting to see Bess Dunbar who'd be returning from collecting Sophy and her granddaughter, Helen, from school.

His fingers strayed to the letter in his pocket and he frowned. I never gave her any encouragement, he told himself. What did she want to write a letter like that for?

He was so preoccupied that Bess and the two children reached him before he realised, but the youngsters weren't surprised to see Uncle Sandy, as they called him. He often met them as they came home from school.

They ran down on to the shore to rake along a line of seaweed while Bess settled herself beside him on the bench and they watched the antics of a noisy oyster-catcher.

'Isn't he bonnie, Bess? Oh, but isn't he bonnie!' He transferred his gaze to her face. 'And you're bonnie! My, it's good to see you with your lovely smile!'

She tilted her head and looked at him with humour lurking in her very blue eyes.

'It's good to see you, too, Sandy.' She laughed. 'But I see you every day. What's brought this on?'

Before he could answer, her eyes darted to the children.

'Helen! Sophy! If you're determined to pull that wood out of the wrack, watch out for nails, you might get hurt!'

He liked to look at her sitting there, animatedly watching the children. Bess didn't have a skinny, fashionable figure.

She was amply rounded in fact, though with neat hips and trim ankles. But it was her lovely expression you took in first. Widowed for a while now, she was unembittered — her face was full of kindness and laughter.

'Now, what's that you were saying, Sandy?' she said distractedly.

'I said you're looking lovely.'

She withdrew her gaze from where the two children were still wrestling with the driftwood and brought it back to search his face.

'You don't seem yourself today, Sandy,' she pronounced. 'You never notice what I look like. What's the matter?'

'Och, I do!' he protested. 'I do notice what you look like — every time we meet. You and I were getting on fine until my sister came back and spoiled it all.'

'Well, you'd no need of my help after Peggy came,' she pointed out. 'She was there to make your soup for you.'

'Nobody makes soup like you, Bess.'

'Now, Sandy — you sound like a wee boy. What is it that's bothering you?'

'I've had a letter from — an admirer,' he admitted after a pause.

He looked so dismayed that it struck Bess as comic and she broke into a peal of such merry laughter that he looked thoroughly offended.

'I was just about to add, don't laugh.' He sighed. 'But I see it would have been a waste of time. Actually I was looking for sympathy.'

'Sympathy?' She chuckled. 'But why? You should be flattered!'

'She wants to marry me,' he said, in the tone of one on whom might have been passed a death sentence.

Catching his mood, Bess sobered. 'I'm sorry I laughed. Obviously this is serious.'

'Not on my part, Bess. I didn't encourage her. You've no idea what it's like being the master of a cruise ship. So many wealthy, unattached women — and you're supposed to be nice to everyone. Some get the wrong idea . . .'

'I can imagine. And you, an un-attached skipper!'

'We were only married a year when Flora died, Bess. I always imagined I'd marry again one day but the years passed . . . And then I retired and came here — and met you, and I thought . . . But I'm too old now, amn't I?'

'Why don't you,' said Bess, 'let this woman be the judge of that?'

'But what will I tell her, this very grand Mrs Ingersoll-Levine, with her mansion in the south, her horses and her fashion clothes? I can't be rude to a lady!'

'Tell her you're very sorry, but you've just got engaged to a fine Highland lady.'

'Bess! You're so wise. I knew if I could just bring my problem to you, you would know what to do. Will you marry me, Bess?' he asked suddenly.

'Oh, Sandy!' Bess laughed. 'I'll not be your scapegoat.'

So Close . . .

Marie was enjoying the drive down to Glasgow in Keir's comfortable car. She looked out at the hills and lochs as they travelled, drinking in the striking scenery.

'It's as lovely as a story-book.'

'Better — it's real! Do you sometimes wish you were back in the city, Marie?' he asked. 'The scenery is beautiful here, but when you're young, the city lights often call.'

She turned towards him, studying his face while he concentrated on the road.

'Well, yes, I do. I was brought up in the city. But it depends on where your heart is — doesn't it?'

'Oh?'

'Well, I mean, if you loved someone very much, and that person worked in the country — like, say, a farmer — you'd only be happy there — wouldn't you?' She smiled winningly at him.

'Would you? Doesn't it depend on the person? Or on the depth of that love?'

She looked thoughtful. 'You sound cynical.'

'Possibly,' he acknowledged.

'Disillusioned?' she hazarded.

'How much do you know about me?' he asked, almost wearily.

'I heard that you're divorced,' she said honestly. 'What happened?'

The blunt question made him frown and it was a long time before he spoke.

'You touched a raw spot talking about relationships depending on where your heart lies,' he conceded. 'I got tired of being a university lecturer. I wanted to get back into the field, which meant sometimes living in fairly remote spots. My ex-wife hated those quiet places — and quite often she'd simply take off for town. Sometimes I'd come home from work and find her gone.' He shrugged expressively. 'Perhaps it wasn't the country — but me — that her heart wasn't in.'

'No, no!' she hastened to reassure him. 'I'm sure it wasn't that. You'd be out at work all the time and she'd be bored, perhaps. If you were in the university post when you married she must have thought . . . '

'She'd married a university.' He laughed mirthlessly.

'That she'd always have a city life,' she persisted.

The car picked up speed on a long straight stretch of road and they were silent for a while.

'I thought, after our child was born, that everything would change.'

'You have a child?' Marie stared at him, astonished.

'Had. He would have been six today — if he'd lived.' His voice was bitter and Marie felt a painful lump form in her throat.

'Oh, Keir! I'm so sorry!'

His hands were clenched on the steering-wheel, the knuckles showing white through the tanned skin. After a few moments, though, he seemed to relax.

'We'll have lunch at Ballachulish, shall we?' he said, though his cheerfulness sounded forced.

'Lovely!' Her voice was soft. 'Was your little boy quite young when he died?' she couldn't resist asking.

He sighed. 'I suppose I'd better finish the story, since I started it, though I don't usually talk about it.' He paused, then went on: 'He was one year old when he contracted meningitis. His mother wasn't home and I couldn't contact her. Any time she'd left us like that, I'd thought she'd gone to her mother's in Newcastle — but she wasn't there. That's when I learned that she'd never been in the habit of going there.' He shook his head. 'All those years . . . '

There was no sound for a while but the hum of the engine.

'When she turned up again it was all over,' he said in a flat voice. 'At the funeral there was just me and the minister, the doctor, the baby's nurse and a few friends from my marine work.'

'She didn't even go to the funeral? How could a mother neglect her own baby like that?' declared Marie. 'It's — it's not natural!'

'There was another man, of course,' he said heavily. 'But it was all a long time ago now.'

'You'll meet someone else,' she told him bracingly.

'Never! I never want to get involved with anyone again.'

★ ★ ★

Chestnut hair shining in the sunlight, Marie hastened up Woodside Crescent, smiling with pleasure when two young men who were sweeping the road leaned on their brushes and whistled as she skipped up on to the high kerb.

She made her way along several of the early Victorian terraces that spread across the hill west of Charing Cross before she found the one she wanted.

She mounted the six shallow steps that arched above the basement entrance and rang one of the bells outside the door.

Roger Ellis, the actor/director she had met at the drama festival, was expecting her and came down in person to open the door and greet her.

He ushered her into a spacious hall and smiled as she gazed around, taking in the rich woodwork of the doors and banister.

'I don't have it all.' He laughed. 'Only the first floor.'

'I wonder if I'll ever have a flat in such a nice place?' she mused wistfully.

'Of course you will. It's this way — up the stairs. I'm pleased that you decided to come!' he said as they went into his living room. 'Do sit down. Did you have a pleasant journey?'

She seated herself in the corner of a long settee set at right angles to the fireplace and he took a seat opposite.

'It was fine, thanks. I came by car. A

friend, Keir McMaster — my boss, actually — happened to be driving down to Glasgow, so he gave me a lift.'

'Cocooned all that way in a car with your boss?' He laughed, teasing her, putting her at her ease.

That's exactly what it had been like, she thought. Cocooned, and pampered. What if life could always be like that?

But although she had flirted outrageously with him he hadn't kissed her. She'd thought there might be an opportunity — but there hadn't.

'Let's have some tea and then get down to business, shall we?' Roger Ellis stood up. 'I only have to boil the kettle.' He waved a hand to where a tea tray stood prepared on a side table.

As he poured boiling water into the teapot, she gazed about her at this glorious room, noticing the raised part which seemed like a little stage with its grand piano.

'I find it useful.' He followed her gaze as he brought the tray, set it before her and joined her on the sofa. 'When I do private tutoring this place is ideal.'

Suddenly Marie felt herself panicking. If he helps me prepare for the auditions, ought I to offer to pay him? she worried. And how do I ask?

'So you're going to audition?' Roger smiled at her, handing her her tea. 'And you have the papers from the college telling you what you have to do? Have you chosen the pieces yet?'

She looked at him helplessly, her eyes troubled.

'Actually I'd like your help in deciding the classic pieces. Do you think Shakespeare or Chekhov?'

'Let me think — is there a two or three-minute soliloquy in 'The Three Sisters'? We don't want to do something everyone does, though. What about the modern piece?'

Marie could feel she was out of her depth.

'Do Shaw and Wilde count as modern?' she asked rather helplessly.

'I believe so. Drink up your tea and we'll get some plays out and look at them. Wilde's got some good parts for women. So has Shaw. We want something that's exactly right for you.'

He saw her beginning to relax. She was very young, but he had a hunch about her . . .

* * *

'I've asked Bess to marry me,' Sandy announced without preamble, and Peggy let out a long high-pitched scream.

'Good heavens, woman! Have you sat on a pin?' he demanded.

His sister had indeed sat down heavily on a chair, her eyes wide, her face white as she stared at him.

Sandy looked at her with a gleam of mischief in his eyes.

'I thought you'd be pleased,' he observed mildly. 'I'm an awful nuisance to you, I'm sure!'

She made a choking sound and glared at him where he had taken up his favourite stance with his back to the fire and his hands clasped behind him.

Taut with resentment, her eyes searched his face.

'And I suppose she jumped at the chance!' she spat out.

His colour deepened at her sarcasm but he managed to speak calmly.

'She didn't jump — no. You couldn't say that she jumped.' His smile was mysterious.

'I suppose I don't look after you well enough?' she commented in a resentful tone.

'I didn't need you to come,' he returned. 'It was your idea to come back here to look after me when I retired.'

She drew herself up and assumed a haughty manner.

'As a matter of fact, my friend in Inverness has often asked me to share her house. And here was I refusing — only out of consideration for you!'

He shrugged. 'Well, there's nothing to stop you. There never was. I believe you're more of a townie nowadays anyway. You're always away to Inverness or somewhere.'

Her foot was tapping out an angry tattoo on the floor.

'First you give Alison the flat — '

'Only temporarily,' he reminded her. 'I'm sure Alison will look for a house for herself and Sophy soon enough. 'You'd no interest in the flat, anyway.'

He stood looking down at her and sighed.

'You always were trouble,' he commented. 'You always wanted to have your cake and eat it. You want the flat kept for you — but you don't want it now. You want to stay in this house — but you don't want the trouble of my callers. You'd like fine to go to Inverness — but you can't make up your mind. So, you use me as an excuse. Well, let me say this again — Bess or no, I do not need looking after!'

She made to protest but he hadn't finished.

'I always meant to marry again. Now you, Peggy, you were just fed up with your work and made an excuse to come home.' He shook his head and sighed. 'Ah, Peggy, Peggy, honesty is a lovely thing. Why not get acquainted with it?'

Her expression was unreadable, her voice cool when she spoke.

'I'll go to Inverness then, since I'm wanted there. It's what you want me to do.'

'No, no, lassie. Do what *you* want to do. You're welcome to stay here. You know that.'

She bridled. 'I'll not stay here with a new mistress in the house. Bess Dunbar. Huh! She always wanted you!'

'That's funny,' her brother mused. 'I wonder why she turned me down then?'

★　★　★

Marie's time in Glasgow seemed to fly by and all too soon it was the day of her audition.

She approached the Royal Scottish Academy of Music and Drama trembling with nerves, yet, at the same time, feeling oddly confident, her head held high.

She had memorised the texts that Roger Ellis had helped her choose, rehearsed them for a week with him and together they had devised appropriate stage movements.

The pieces were to be performed to a special panel.

In her first piece, Marie was Irena from Chekhov's 'The Three Sisters'. Roger Ellis had suggested the lines for the different shades of emotion they had to express. As Irena she was first glowing and lovely, then turbulent — and finally pathetic.

Irena is twenty. The hope that sustains her in her unsatisfactory life is that of returning to live in Moscow but she realises this will never happen.

Marie's confidence grew as she performed the emotional scene.

'I've been waiting all this time, imagining that we'd be moving to Moscow, and I'd meet the man I'm meant for there. I've dreamt about him and I've loved him in my dreams. But it's all turned out to be nonsense . . . nonsense . . . '

When she had finished she was surprised to find her cheeks wet with real tears and turned to wipe them away.

A dark head had been in her mind's eye — Keir McMaster had filled her imagination.

The panel had greeted the end of her speech with complete silence and she had no idea whether it was a good sign or not. She watched them muttering between themselves and making notes on their pads, and then she was asked to perform her next piece.

Roger Ellis had insisted that it should contrast sharply with the first and show some breadth to her acting potential.

Now she was Mother Courage in Brecht's play — haggard, worn-out, struggling to stay alive in a war-torn land, to wrest some kind of living for herself and her children.

It was a very different part from

Irena. Should she have done them in the other order? She felt herself an inadequate Mother Courage.

Before her performances, she'd had a limbering up session led by the movement tutor to assess suppleness. Now she had to reproduce notes sounded on the piano by the voice tutor.

Then came the questions, about why she had chosen the pieces, her reasons for applying to the college, what she would do with the training. There were more questions about theatre, acting, drama in the community. Why hadn't she come straight from school? What were her educational qualifications?

Her mind was whirling, but she was given no indication of how she had fared, but was simply told to return at twelve-thirty to take part in a group improvisation session.

When she emerged from the interview, she found Roger Ellis waiting for her in the entrance hall and he took her off for coffee to calm her nerves. After the improvisation session, he promised, he would return and reward her for her strenuous morning by taking her to his club for lunch.

Six other prospective students took part with her in the improvisation session and, as before, Marie had little idea of how they had all got on.

Over lunch, Roger Ellis wanted more details of her morning. What did she think of the college, the people, the atmosphere?

Relief that it was finally all over made her light-hearted and she replied with spirited excitement, and he leaned back in his chair, contemplating her vivid face with pleasure, basking in the admiring glances directed her way by the other men in the room. He was sure he'd backed a winner.

'How can I repay you for your help?' she managed to ask at last.

He shrugged. 'Just by doing your best.'

'Don't you — I don't know — submit an account?' she asked uneasily.

She found it embarrassing to be asking if she should pay him, but she didn't want to appear stupid if that was what he expected, if that was the done thing.

He shook his head, his mouth widening in a grin.

'No charge. I have confidence in you,' he said. Then he rocked forward on his chair suddenly, looking deeply into her eyes. 'This Keir McMaster — you imagine you're in love with him, don't you? Where does that leave us?'

She turned pale with the suddenness of his accusation and then the colour swept into her face.

'I — yes, I think I do love him.' She looked at him almost defiantly. 'Is there something that says you can't be in love *and* be an actor?'

He burst out laughing. 'You're a game one!' and his look was full of admiration. 'As a matter of fact, you'll never be an actress of worth till you have been in love — preferably unrequited. You'll be a better one still when you've suffered far worse. You haven't lived yet, child. But, when you do — ' He nodded several times: ' — I have high hopes for you.'

★   ★   ★

'Look, Mum! Look! See? It's a baby seal lying on the rock!' Sophy jumped up and down with excitement.

'Don't go near it, pet. If you do its mother might be frightened away. She's sure to have left it there while she's off fishing. If you watch carefully you'll spot her out there soon. She'll keep bobbing up to see how her baby is doing. Let's just move farther along the beach so's not to disturb them.'

Alison and Sophy had been at the field station for just a few days. A post-graduate student was due to join them, but she hadn't arrived yet.

Sophy occupied herself by digging in the wet sand while Alison finished making her notes and began scanning the sea through binoculars. After a few minutes she sighed. She had no intention of telling Sophy at this stage, but she could see no sign of a common seal mother out in the water. She would have to keep watch at least through the turn of the tide, or even longer, before deciding if the little seal had in fact been abandoned.

'I'm sure the mummy seal's not out there. I've been looking!' Sophy announced irrepressibly. 'Couldn't I just go and get the pup and make a little pool for it?'

Alison sighed. 'You must never handle a baby seal you see on the beach, Sophy. Promise me you won't. They're such friendly little things it would follow you. We'd never get it back to its mother and then it would die.'

'Couldn't we feed it?'

'I wish we could, pet, but that's just the trouble. The mother's milk is so rich and complex it's almost impossible to substitute.'

She scanned the water again through her glasses. There was an inflatable dinghy out there now — but not a trace of a seal watching the shore.

'Let's have some tea, shall we?' She jumped up. 'I'll bring it down from the caravan. You wait here. And remember, you're not to go near the baby. All right?'

Sophy nodded and went back to her digging.

Alison filled a flask with tea, added two mugs and biscuits and was bringing the basket back down the beach when she halted. A man in diving gear was coming out of the water near the seal's rock and Sophy was running towards him, waving and shouting, 'Go away! Go away!'

The man didn't retreat but raised his arms in a gesture of surrender.

His hair looked black, sleeked down with water. It wasn't until he pulled off his snorkel and mask that she recognised him. It was Keir McMaster.

She hurried towards him, struggling to control her rapid heartbeats and the quickening of her pulse.

'Sophy didn't want the baby seal disturbed,' she explained hurriedly. 'I've been explaining that its mother will be watching.'

'Oh!' He stood before her, water still dripping from his wet-suit encased body. 'I thought you'd been training her to see all men off!'

'It's not a bad idea,' she returned. 'I have been singularly unfortunate in the ones I've known.'

He started to move away from the rock with them.

'Isolation depressing you?' he asked casually.

'A reasonable degree of isolation doesn't depress me. I'm not sure, though, that it's an ideal situation for a child. Children need other children.'

'She has her mother,' he returned.

Sophy bounded ahead of them, excited by Keir's unexpected appearance, and he watched her progress thoughtfully.

'There might be a solution to the isolation at least. We've had word of more post-graduates coming. It would depend on their experience.'

'Don't worry about that,' she said coolly. 'I don't make a practice of ducking out of my commitments.'

'Don't you? And do you count your marriage as a commitment?'

For a moment she was speechless at his effrontery and then she rallied.

'What on earth do you mean by that?'

'Oh, nothing.' He shrugged dismissively. 'I suppose I was just thinking how often I see you in Gavin Dunbar's company.'

'Gavin — and his mother — is a very good neighbour. I don't know what I would have done without the Dunbars' help and support!' Even as she protested, she wondered crossly why she was troubling to defend her actions to this man.

'I didn't realise that being my boss included assuming responsibility for my moral and spiritual welfare,' she continued. 'How Victorian! Would you like a run-down of my prayer list now?'

Her eyes were afire with fury as she stamped ahead of him, still carrying the basket.

A few long strides brought him to her side again.

'Am I on it?' he asked.

'On what?'

'Your prayer list?'

'You've need to be!'

She slammed the basket down on the sand and knelt beside it.

'Tea?' she asked as he flopped nearby.

'Do you generally give tea to your enemies?'

'Yes, even those that despitefully use me.' She twisted the flask-top off savagely and, using it as a third cup, poured out the tea.

'Thanks.' He took it gratefully.

Sophy, to Alison's disgust, sat at his feet, and as if to compensate, Alison herself moved farther away, establishing a distance between herself and his muscular body.

'We're sure the mother's lost,' Sophy

confided in him, determined not to be drawn from the topic that filled her mind.

'We're not sure at all!' Alison hastily corrected her. 'Dr McMaster knows all about seals, Sophy. He'll tell you not to disturb them, too.'

And now, after his infuriating remarks to her, Keir was responding to Sophy with exceptional kindness.

'The glimpse I got of your orphan — if it is one — made me think it was dehydrated. Did you notice the dark rings round its eyes?'

As Sophy nodded earnestly, he sent a questioning glance to Alison over the child's head and she nodded, too.

He looked away over the white sand and abruptly back to her again, as though seeing her for the first time.

She had on a powder-blue cotton top. Her magnolia skin had a new healthy glow and her auburn waves were hopelessly disarrayed. She looked elfin — and, somehow, elusive.

Wanting to speak to him without

Sophy hearing, Alison raised her eyes to his and surprised an odd look in his eyes, an expression she couldn't read on his face, but he seemed to read her thoughts.

'Sophy!' He laid a gentle hand on the child's hair. 'Could you find me some cockleshells that haven't been broken? I've got a student at the station who's doing some drawings and she needs very special ones.'

As Sophy leapt up, eager to help, and rushed down to the tideline, Keir turned to Alison.

'Should I just take a quick look at the charts before I go?'

'Yes.' She gathered up the tea things and led him over the deserted shore to the grassy stretch behind them where the two station caravans were parked in a small fenced-in enclosure.

'Could you bring some things over to me?' she asked, hating having to be dependent on him.

His nearness, his intense masculinity, disturbed her and she stepped back abruptly. She seemed to be perpetually distancing herself from this man.

'I'll need a liquidiser — '

'Having a friend for dinner?' he quipped.

Alison sighed in exasperation.

'Hardly! If the baby seal turns out to be an orphan, I'll need to feed it liquidised fish. It doesn't look as though it's been fed since birth. And if it is an orphan, it'll be too late if I don't have everything ready.'

'How long are you going to wait for its mother?'

'Till the morning.'

'It looked pretty poorly,' he warned her and she sighed.

'I know. But I'd never forgive myself if the mother returned and found her pup gone! And then — it's Sophy, you see . . . ' How could she explain that Sophy was hoping for some kind of pet since her cat had disappeared into the Torquillan hills?

'I know. After losing her cat.'

She looked at him in amazement,

surprised that he could be so perceptive and understanding. Her heart-shaped face was earnest as she gazed at him, and both were very aware of the tension between them.

'I doubt if the seal will survive,' he said after a pause.

'We'll see. I'll need antibiotics and a range of vitamins. Oh, and fish. How will I catch the fish I'll need . . . ?'

'And how will you get the nourishment into the pup . . . ?'

They returned to the beach discussing what could be done for the seal.

Sophy had been watching for them and ran up to Keir with the shells she had collected for him, and he thanked her with amazing charm, smiling down into her eager little face.

'I'll get off now . . . ' he began to say when there was a loud shout from the hill behind them.

Sophy was first to recognise the figure.

'It's Gavin!' she squealed and dashed off in the direction of the figure striding down the hill.

'Well, goodbye.' Keir was suddenly formal. 'I won't keep you from your guest.' His eyes were cold. 'And I'll see that you get your liquidiser.'

He waded into the water until it was deep enough for him to start swimming towards the dinghy — while she stood looking after him, an inexplicable despair in her heart.

Marooned!

Alison watched until she saw Keir McMaster hoist himself into the dinghy, then she turned away from the sea to scan the hillside for Gavin.

She should be pleased to see him appearing so unexpectedly, she told herself, so why was she experiencing this inner turmoil?

'Gavin!' She waved enthusiastically and hurried after Sophy who was clambering up to meet him.

There was no road down this side of the loch, only miles of old, uncertain forest track which at one time had served a farm. The field station's electricity supply came via a cable from the old farm.

Sophy had reached him now and she squealed in delight as he caught her up in his arms and swung her round.

'What are you doing here?' Alison

called as she scrambled up towards them.

He set Sophy on her feet and took both of Alison's hands in his as she reached him.

'Are you all right?' His eyes seemed to search her soul.

'All right? Yes! Yes, of course! Why do you ask?'

'Oh, no reason. Was that your boss leaving? Swimming away like a mythical god?'

His sarcasm acted like a tonic and she let out a peal of laughter.

'Oh, Gavin, you are awful!'

He grinned. 'Well! What the heck does he think he's doing, dumping you here like this?'

'Oh, there's no question about what he's doing!' She laughed. 'He's trying to prove that I won't measure up to the man he wanted for the job. I, however, am determined to prove him wrong! Anyway, how did you get here?'

'By jeep. I'm doing a survey over here — at least, that's my story! But, to be honest, it was just an excuse to see if you're OK. It's so far by road!'

'But not by water,' she pointed out.

'I'm not that fond of water,' he admitted.

'Gavin.' Sophy reached up for his hand. 'There's a baby seal over there. Come and see.'

'Sophy! Not again! I told you, we must leave it alone.' Alison sighed. 'Come on, Gavin — come and have some lunch with us.'

'I've got my own sandwiches but I'll have your company and some coffee.'

Alison led the way across the grassy raised beach to the caravan site, and pointed to a small area beside the laboratory, enclosed by chicken-net.

'Gavin, could I ask you to check that enclosure for us, in case we do have the seal here? Would you have time?'

'I'll make time since it's for you!'

While she boiled a kettle inside, he tested each of the supports in turn, then popped his head round the door to report in.

'There are some shaky posts but it's nothing major. I'll fetch some tools from the jeep after lunch and fix them. I'll see that Sophy has the most glamorous seal-enclosure in the west!' he joked.

'She might not have a seal, though,' Alison cautioned, still hoping that the seal would be claimed by its mother.

'She can have the place for a garden then, or a hen-coop — any number of things. It must have been made for something — another seal by the looks of it.'

They sat down on the grass outside to eat their lunch.

'So — what's new?' Alison wanted to know.

'Marie's back.' Gavin bit into his cheese and pickle sandwich.

'Oh? How did the audition go?'

'All right, I think. She didn't have time to tell me much.'

She looked at him speculatively.

'You like Marie, don't you, Gavin?'

He turned his gaze away to the peaks

of the islands out in the Atlantic.

'Ay, I like her,' he admitted. 'Have you ever seen anything like her, Alison? They must have broken the mould . . . But, if she has her way, she'll have McMaster. Though I hope she doesn't.'

Alison snorted. 'I shouldn't worry. He seems to loathe all women. Anyway, won't Marie be moving to Glasgow if she gets offered a place at drama college?'

'To be honest, I don't think she knows what she'll do.'

'She's young,' Alison commented, smiling reassuringly at him.

'You had Sophy when you were her age,' he pointed out.

'I know.' Alison gazed out to sea and nodded thoughtfully. 'It made me grow up quickly — being suddenly responsible for a child. You're never young again.'

'Do you regret it?'

She shook her head.

'I couldn't regret having Sophy . . . But I'm glad my father made me complete my degree. You never know what's ahead of you.'

Sophy finished her lunch and turned to her mother.

'Mum! Can I go and get buckets of water from the sea and start to fill that plastic tank? Then it'll be ready for the baby seal.'

'Yes, if you like — but, Sophy . . . ' She was about to sound a warning note but Gavin interrupted.

'Off you go,' he said. 'You'll need more water than you can carry — but you could start. Everything to hand?' he asked Alison as Sophy pottered off.

'Except the right nourishment,' she said, frowning.

'Forget about that just now,' he said, watching as Sophy ran down to the shoreline with a bucket. 'I've been wanting to talk to you alone — about us — you and me.'

He looked into her eyes and she drew back a little.

'Gavin! Even if — '

'Even if there was some definite news

of your husband's death?' he supplied. 'And what if there was? Is there any chance for us together?'

She shook her head sadly.

'Not now, Gavin. Our romance was over long ago. We were only teenagers, remember.'

'But I still care for you, Alison.' He smiled gently. 'And I like Sophy, too. We get on great.'

'I know. You're marvellous with her and she adores you. But, Gavin, you're being silly. It's Marie you really want.'

'I thought it was, but she seems — beyond my grasp somehow,' he admitted honestly.

'So what you're saying is that, even if I was free — I'd always be your second best?'

'No! Oh, I don't know! Anyway, I can't have Marie!'

'How do you know? Have you asked her?' When he shook his head, she nodded with satisfaction. 'There you go then! What about the Lifeboat Dance tomorrow night? There's your chance.

Take her for a stroll in the moonlight,'
she suggested.

'Take her for a stroll?' He groaned. 'I
can't get near her! I'd have to queue
up!' Then he looked thoughtful. 'Is
there a moon tomorrow night?'

★ ★ ★

'Those are big pearls hanging from
your ears, pet!' Agnes's thin hand
reached up to touch the giant baubles
in her granddaughter's ears.

'They're not real ones, Gran. They're
just for fun,' Marie said.

'Talk about gilding the lily!' Aunt Isa
scooped bacon and eggs, mushrooms
and fried pancakes on to the plates.
'You're decked out like a Christmas
tree, girl. And if ever I saw a lassie that
didn't need to bother, it's you.'

Marie blushed with pleasure. 'I've
never heard you so kind! Thank you!'

'Thank me nothing. I wasn't con-
gratulating you for it. It's just luck. You
were just fortunate to be born beautiful!

And what's all this glamour for tonight then?' Isa asked.

'I'm just deciding what to wear for the Lifeboat Dance tomorrow.'

'Oh? I took a ticket myself — just to support it. But I might come along. I can always give a hand in the kitchen if they're not queueing up to dance with me!' She turned to Agnes. 'You'd be all right for an hour on your own, Mother, wouldn't you?' she asked loudly.

'I'll be going. Hamish and I always go to the Lifeboat Dance,' Mrs McPhail announced. 'I'll wear the long black velvet frock my sister sent from Glasgow.'

'Yes, Mother. That's the one you should wear,' Isa said, gently humouring the old lady's step back into a past long gone. 'But you're thinking about the big Lifeboat Ball in the winter — this is just a wee hop for the visitors.'

Isa turned back to her niece.

'And who are you going with, Marie?'

Marie shrugged. 'Nobody special. I'm just going with some girls from the drama club. But who knows who'll be taking me home?' she added coyly.

'Who's taking you home tonight,' Mrs McPhail began to sing, 'after the ball is over?'

'Why, Mother! That's marvellous! Imagine you being able to remember that old song!' Isa laughed delightedly and began to join in with her own rendition of the old refrain: 'Who's the lucky boy who's going your way? To kiss you goodnight at your doorway?' she crooned, and Marie collapsed in mirth.

'That was never a song?'

'It was! Very popular in the dance halls, it was.'

'No! I love it! And I love you when you're fun like this!' Marie grinned at her aunt. 'It's great here when you're not scolding me. You must have been a lovely girl,' she added more seriously and with one of those rare flashes of sensitive perception which were so unexpected in her.

'Oh, certainly. Where do you think you get your good bones from? It's that wee touch of the Spanish in us — from the Armada, you know.' Isa tilted her head to display her high cheekbones.

'The Spanish Armada,' Mrs McPhail spaced out the words. 'I remember it all right . . .'

'No, no you're thinking of the war, Mum,' Isa said. 'A lot of young men went away from here to the Second World War and never came back.'

Isa began to gather up the used dishes, humming, 'Who's taking you home tonight?' in a soft crooning tone, wrapped up in her own thoughts.

'Lifeboats are a blessing,' remarked Mrs McPhail with a shaft of clarity.

'A car's a blessing coming home from a dance,' Marie observed, tilting back on her chair and stretching hugely. 'I'd rather be kissed in a car than in a doorway.'

'You're too frivolous by far, young lady,' her aunt told her as she poured out their tea. 'Just watch your step!'

* * *

Having kept watch on the baby seal through the change of the tide and till the next morning, Alison was now convinced that the mother was not going to return, so she gently wrapped the pup in an old blanket and carried it to the caravan. It was obviously very weak. There was no saying how long ago its mother had abandoned it.

Sophy ran beside her, begging to be allowed to hold it, but it was in a pitiful state.

'Wait, Sophy — not yet. Maybe when it's a bit better.'

Alison set it down on her plastic mackintosh which she had laid on top of the carpet in the caravan, and trained the ceiling heater on to it to try to warm the poor thing.

Then she tried to get small drops of water into its mouth, longing for the supplies she had asked her boss to bring her.

Sophy was kneeling beside her, willing the pup to respond, when Keir McMaster walked in, startling them with his sudden appearance. His presence seemed to fill the caravan.

'No parent?' he asked abruptly.

Alison looked up at him and shook her head.

'I'm convinced now. Nothing less would have made me move him. If only people wouldn't go near them and frighten away the mother in the first place!'

'I think I've got everything on your list.' He knelt down beside them, appraising the seal. 'It's maybe too late . . . '

'We'll see.' Alison rummaged in the basket of supplies he had brought and when she found the package she wanted, she removed a sachet from it and went for the kettle she had boiled earlier.

'What are you going to do, Mummy?'

'These sachets contain powders to help with dehydration — remember I explained about dehydration? They have special salts and glucose in them. Once I've mixed some with water I'm going to try to get the liquid into the baby . . . We can't keep calling it that! Give it a name, Sophy.'

Sophy fixed her eyes on Dr McMaster as though looking for inspiration.

'Something that comes out of the sea?' he responded. And then he gave her an astonishingly sweet smile. 'Something that sounds like a wet dish-rag?'

'Rag?' she pondered. 'Raggie? Raggie? Dish-mop . . . Mop? Moppy, Floppy!' She giggled.

'All these describe him at the moment,' Alison pointed out, and Sophy nodded.

'But he won't always be a floppy-looking thing, will he? So I'm going to give him a proper, grown-up name,' Sophy announced thoughtfully.

'He might just be a dead seal,' Alison put in brutally, trying to prepare her daughter for the most likely outcome.

Her boss gave her a long steady glance as she stood stirring the liquid but she met his gaze unflinchingly.

'I'm going to call him Fairbairn,' Sophy pronounced.

'Fairbairn? But why?' Two pairs of eyes turned questioningly on her.

Alison began to feed the seal with the special tubing Keir had brought and as he struggled, Sophy put out a finger to touch him.

'Poor Fairbairn!'

'Why Fairbairn?' Keir asked again.

'Well, Mrs Dunbar says the seals are the people of the sea. Bairns are people's children. He's ugly just now. But he's going to be beautiful. He's going to be a fair bairn — you see?' It was astounding logic for a child, and her anxiety to make him understand was palpable.

He returned her serious stare.

'Why, of course I see, now that you've explained it. It's a beautiful name, perfect.'

For some reason, Alison felt a lump in her throat. She sometimes wished her daughter wasn't such an earnest little girl.

'She's been here before,' Keir murmured to her when Sophy's attention was elsewhere — as though he had read her thoughts — and went on, 'Don't worry — she'll be carefree later on.'

She gave him a look of utter astonishment. How on earth did he know that she wanted her daughter to be carefree now — in childhood?

She got up and took the remaining liquid to the work area.

'I brought you a giant syringe to force the liquidised food down its throat.' He spoke to her back. 'When are you starting with the pulverised fish?'

'Soon. I thought tomorrow. It must be nourished quickly.'

'I'll lift him into the laboratory for you later. You can't have him in here. And we can't have him thinking you're his mother!'

Good heavens, had he actually got a sense of humour? As she detected yet another unknown aspect to him, Alison felt it could be a long time before she really got to know this man.

'You mustn't handle him any more than is necessary to feed him — and pop him into the tank of water every day for a while, then try him in the sea — or a pool perhaps to begin with.'

'That's what I thought,' she agreed.

'I didn't have any fish to bring,' he went on, 'but I've been promised some sprat and herring which I'll bring over later.'

'You will?' Her eyes were large with surprise. 'But you could send somebody.'

'Yes. I could, couldn't I? We'll see.'

She followed him down to the shoreline and watched as he dragged the inflatable dinghy into the water, then she and Sophy stood waving to him as he started the outboard motor and sped off in a wide arc towards Torquillan.

As she watched, it occurred to her that this was the first time they had met without squabbling.

Keir returned in the late afternoon,

although by then the sea had roughened and an ominous cloud formation was moving in from the west.

He found Alison working in the laboratory, and as she took the container of fish from him she was thinking aloud.

'I'll skin and bone them and make a paste including some of the vitamins.' She glanced up at him. 'Fairbairn has kept all his liquid food down and seems to be sleeping calmly,' she reported.

She stood at the bench expecting him to leave, but he made no move to go and finally, rather embarrassed by his silent presence, she asked if he would like to come into the other caravan and have a look at the orphan.

'I would.' He stood aside and let her precede him.

$\star$ $\quad$ $\star$ $\quad$ $\star$

They found Sophy 'babysitting', and making up a jigsaw puzzle on a tray, and he joined her on the bench-seat

185

and proceeded to help.

'How's Fairbairn now, Sophy?'

'He's much better,' she reported earnestly. 'We want to keep him in here just one night, don't we, Mummy?'

Alison looked guilty and hastily explained: 'He needs a lamp for a little while. I'm using the heater in place of one just now.'

'You should have said you need a lamp. I'll bring one over and rig it up in the lab.'

'Oh no! You've gone to too much trouble already.'

'I'm interested,' he replied briefly.

She shrugged. 'Oh! Well — I was just going to make a cup of tea. D'you want one?'

'Yes, please. How about this piece, Sophy?' Keir looked at the girl's jigsaw pieces. 'D'you think it's a bit of the roof?'

She peered at it and nodded. 'I think it is. I think I'll put all the roof-coloured pieces together over here.'

He smiled approval. 'You're a very

methodical young lady — and a very clever one, I believe.'

Sophy sighed. 'I'd rather be pretty like Helen.'

'Why not be pretty like yourself?' he commented, smiling kindly at her.

'Here's the tea!' Alison exclaimed quickly to rescue him from a discussion with Sophy about her looks.

The puzzle was put aside till they drank tea and they all looked down at the seal who obligingly opened his beautiful soulful eyes for them. It was a curiously content moment.

However, the mood was broken when a few drops of rain spattered on the windows and a low, moaning wind rose in the trees. Then, with a suddenness that took their breath away, the caravan was rocked by a mighty gust of wind.

Both Alison and Sophy instinctively looked to Keir.

'Looks like we're in for one of those freak storms Torquillan suffers occasionally,' he said calmly, and Alison nodded.

'I remember once when I was a girl here in Torquillan. We went into church one morning and there was no wind but as the service went on we could hear it gathering and when we came out there was a tree down across the road. We could hardly get home against the gale. Funny how you don't get any warning.'

'Not for this. The cloud and rain coming in from the Atlantic were one thing but this is local. The wind's slewed round to the north here.'

'I hope there's nobody out there in a small boat!' Alison observed, getting up to look out of the window at the rising seas. She could see that the trees in the woods behind them appeared to be flattening down like a quilt settling over the ground. 'What's that awful sound?' she asked as a wailing filled the air.

'It's the wind. Eerie, isn't it?'

'I'll say!' she agreed.

Sophy shivered as the noise grew louder. 'I'm frightened!'

'Don't be. You're fine here.' Keir put

his arm round her and, to Alison's astonishment, pulled her comfortingly against his side.

'Aren't you worried about the dinghy?' Alison asked him.

'Only a madman would venture on to the water in this!'

'I know.' She heard her voice sharpening. 'I mean, won't it get blown away?'

'I've pulled it well up and jammed the anchor amongst some rocks.'

She shrugged helplessly. She was anxious for Keir to go. What if the storm continued and he had to stay all night?

'Aren't you going to the dance?' she asked.

'Can you suggest some way I could get there?'

'No. A lifeboat, maybe . . . ' she joked and she saw him grin.

The caravan, shuddering constantly, gave a more violent rock as a gust of wind hit it and Alison grimaced.

'If there's one thing that sets my

nerves on edge, it's the wind,' she confessed, a little shaken.

She looked at Sophy's stricken expression and tried to muster a cheerful smile.

'Come on, Sophy. Let's put on a brave face for Dr McMaster.'

'You'd better call me Keir if I've to be here all night,' he commented.

Hearing her fears voiced, she shivered.

'I couldn't,' she protested.

'Try,' he returned.

She shook her head then swiftly changed the subject.

'I'd better get some food ready,' she said. 'I wonder what I can make without getting scalded?'

'Sandwiches?' he suggested.

'Well, yes. We've got tins of salmon and cold meats. And there's some salad — ' She paused, catching sight of her daughter's distressed face. 'Oh, love, don't cry! It's only the wind.'

'I don't know why I'm crying,' Sophy sniffed.

'I expect it is the wind.' Keir held her closer. 'But don't cry! We're going to have something to eat and then we'll play some games to pass the time. What games have you here? Here — let me dry your eyes while you tell me.'

She let him mop her face with a large handkerchief while she reeled off the games she had brought with her.

'There's Scrabble . . . '

'Scrabble would be good, only the letters might get thrown about. Let's play 'The Minister's Cat' while Mummy gets the supper. I'll say, the Minister's cat is an abominable cat . . . '

However, at that Sophy burst in to a fresh storm of tears.

'I want Tabitha to come home!' she wailed, remembering her cat which had disappeared into Torquillan's hills.

As Keir McMaster looked at her helplessly, guilt and dismay etched on his features, Alison felt like weeping, too. The constant tension of trying to care for her daughter and do her work well sometimes stretched her nerves to breaking point.

The caravan gave another frightening shudder and they all flinched. Alison was certain it would be blown over as she filled the kettle and water splashed over her hands and arms.

Keir was watching her.

'I should never have sent you here,' he said. 'You'll come back with me tomorrow and I'll send someone else.'

'You will not!'

'What do you mean?'

'I mean I won't give up now. You think I'm not capable of coping with the job.'

'It's not that. I know you're more than capable . . . '

'In that case you're making an emotional — rather than a professional — judgement,' she protested.

As the wind howled with renewed fury, Sophy buried her head in Keir's fisherman's jersey, and he looked up helplessly.

'Look, I can't argue with you in this

wind,' he admitted. 'I'll tell you later.'

His statement was like a red rag to a bull.

'Oh, so you'll tell me! We won't *discuss* it later — you'll just tell me!' she yelled and she saw a warning flash in his eyes.

'Hush!' He indicated the top of Sophy's curls and she felt a pang of guilt. The poor child was upset enough without hearing this.

Abruptly she turned away from him.

'I have to feed Fairbairn again.'

'Sophy and I will hold him. Won't we, Sophy?'

At the mention of the seal, Sophy seemed to become calmer.

'If you manage to revive him,' he went on, as Fairbairn was fed, 'I wouldn't mind taking him over to the concrete pool at the station to swim and feed there till he grows bigger. He'd be an attraction for children to watch. And one of the students might like to study his progress.'

Once they'd fed the seal, they ate the

sandwiches Alison had prepared. Even as they had their scratch meal, Sophy grew more and more sleepy and finally, in spite of the noise all around them, she dozed off.

Alison wanted to carry her through to the double berth next door but Keir insisted she sleep on the bench-seat beside them in case she awoke and was frightened.

After Sophy had fallen asleep they spoke in undertones though the storm continued to rage loudly outside.

'Why not go through to bed yourself and get some rest?' he suggested. 'I'll stay here beside Sophy.'

She shook her head.

'What shall we do then?' His eyes looked wicked. 'Play Scrabble? Talk?'

'I can't bear it,' she said suddenly. 'Why did this have to happen?'

After The Storm

The Lifeboat Dance was going with a swing, the band playing a Highland Scottische. Gavin was dancing with Marie, and every time it came to the birling, he swung her up in his arms and whirled her round and round.

She laughed, she sparkled, seemingly tireless. She was well aware that the night was half gone and that Keir McMaster hadn't turned up. But she wasn't going to let anyone guess that she minded.

She danced every dance, her earrings swinging gaily.

Sandy Matheson had taken the tickets at the door and was now free to go and see how Bess and the rest of the helpers were getting on in the kitchen.

He found his sister taking sandwiches out of boxes and bags and placing them on plates to be handed round, but as he yielded to the temptation to take a sandwich off one of the plates, Peggy slapped his hand.

'You'll wait like everyone else!'

'Och, Peggy, give him one,' said the gentle Bess, busy slicing up cake. 'Give him two.'

'You would, I know,' snapped Peggy, causing deeper colour to run up into Bess's pink cheeks.

Peggy knew Sandy was sweet on Bess but she'd never been close to the other woman.

Sandy sent Bess an apologetic look, affection in his eyes. There might be a waltz later, and he hoped to dance it with her . . .

Marie took supper with a group of the youngsters but Gavin made sure he was sitting beside her.

'Who's taking you home?' he whispered under cover of the general merriment.

To his surprise, she collapsed into a fit of the giggles.

'What are you laughing at?' he wanted to know, ready to be offended.

'Oh — I'm not laughing at you! It's a song Gran and Aunt Isa were singing yesterday, that's all!'

Marie had another look round the hall. It was obvious now that Keir wasn't coming. Perhaps she should let Gavin run her home; certainly she didn't want to have to walk!

'Come on, Gavin — a Pride of Erin. And look who's got your mother up for it,' she said as she spotted Sandy dancing with Bess.

'Help, Marie — I'm exhausted!' he protested. 'Where do you get the energy?'

'Och, lazy-bones! Well, you sit there — I'm going to make Aunt Isa come and dance it with me!'

She skimmed across the floor and pulled her aunt out of her chair and into the dance.

★　★　★

'Bess,' Sandy whispered, 'now I've got you in my arms at last, have you changed your mind about marrying me yet?'

'Now, Sandy! You're taking an unfair advantage — asking me to dance and then starting to tease me again!'

'I'm not teasing, lass. I'm in deadly earnest.'

She looked at him intently.

'We're too old to change our ways.'

He looked indignant. 'You might be but I'm not. I'm just a boy!' he protested, and she couldn't help laughing. 'But have you thought about it, Bess?' he persisted.

'I don't want to be anybody's housekeeper,' she said, looking thoughtful. 'I've had a busy enough life. Anyway, what about Peggy?'

'Who said anything about housekeeper? I can hire a housekeeper if I want one,' he told her firmly. 'Is Peggy the trouble . . . ?'

She shrugged. 'Peggy — Gavin — a whole lot of things are the trouble. Me . . . '

'Bess, forget everyone else and obey your heart. That's what I've decided to do at long last. And if I'm mistaken about us . . . I'll not torment you, mo ghaoil, I promise.'

Bess blinked tears out of her eyes and swallowed a little lump in her throat. It was a long time since anyone had spoken so tenderly to her. Surely she wasn't getting soft — and maybe feeling a wee bit tired of always being taken for granted?

Mind you, there was a warm feeling about being swung round the dance floor in Sandy Matheson's strong arms.

★　★　★

Gavin brought his pick-up to the door so that Marie wouldn't get soaked reaching it through the storm. His hair was plastered to his head in the seconds it had taken to reach his vehicle and the door he held open for her was almost blown out of his hands.

'So much for romance in the moonlight!' he exclaimed in disgust.

'What?' she yelled above the howling wind.

'Nothing!' He felt his cause doomed before he had started.

He drove her straight home. There would be no joy in driving to the lovers' favourite spot. The sea was coming right over the road.

She let him kiss her goodnight but he knew her heart wasn't in it.

'It's always been you I've liked, Marie,' he told her.

'You say that to everyone,' she protested.

'How do you know?'

'I know everything.' She smiled.

'Then you know I love you.'

'I know you're the biggest flirt in Torquillan!'

'Aw, Marie! You're in a cruel mood tonight, but I'm not giving up!'

'Please yourself. Is Sandy taking my aunt and your mother home?'

'Yes. They're going back to our house

for a blether first. Let's just go and join them.'

'No, thanks. If you don't mind, I think I'll just go in and see how my gran's getting on.' She opened the car door.

'Some of the lads from the marine station were saying that Keir McMaster had gone across the loch with some fish Alison wanted,' he told Marie to prevent her leaving. He succeeded.

'He what?' She closed the door again with a bang. 'So that's where he is!' Anger made her breathing uneven. 'But he said he'd be at the dance!'

Gavin was half sorry he had stirred things up. It was doing nothing for his cause.

'He could hardly get back in this!' he protested.

She took several deep breaths to control herself.

'I just hope he didn't set off back before the gale struck,' she commented.

He felt there were tears of anxiety in

her voice and regretted his words still more.

'I'm sure he didn't,' he said to calm her. And then the imp of mischief in him took over again. 'But wouldn't that be preferable to having him isolated with the gorgeous Alison?'

For a moment she looked as though she would like to hit him, but then she again took control of her emotions, breathing deeply.

'I'd rather that than any harm come to him,' she said quietly, then wrenched the door open again. ''Bye, Gavin. Thanks for the lift. I'm sorry for poor Alison and Sophy over there in this gale — aren't you anxious about them?' she added pointedly.

Let him worry for a change.

* * *

Sophy continued to sleep peacefully under the blanket Keir had gently draped over her as the night wore on but Alison's tension simply increased.

She felt a strange panic gathering in her. She wished she could walk away — though it wasn't even possible to walk up and down in the confines of the caravan without disturbing Sophy. She told herself she hated being cooped up with this insufferable man. She wished he hadn't been so tender with Sophy. She tried to stop her heart warming to him for that.

She couldn't admit that the tall, athletic body, the bronzed face and stern eyes stirred in her old longings that she had no right to feel — that she had thought quenched for ever.

'What's the matter?' He eyed her quizzically.

'Nothing. It's the wind — it always gets to me.'

He got up and brought the Scrabble and placed the board on the bench-seat between them and they played as best they could. Sometimes there appeared to be a lull in the wind before another fierce blast would rock the caravan and send the letters flying.

After one such disaster he put the game aside and took her hand.

'What's the matter?' he said again. 'You're as nervous as a cat!'

She shivered. 'I don't know.' She looked up into his face, into his dark eyes and felt she was lost. She felt she had no resistance left . . .

He bent his head and his mouth gently touched hers. Alison knew she ought to pull away — but she couldn't. How could a man she hated rouse such emotion in her?

She closed her eyes, losing herself in the sweet bliss of his caress.

After a long moment, he raised his head.

'I'm sorry. I didn't mean to do that. I know I shouldn't have,' he whispered.

She had a hysterical desire to thank him for kissing her, though she wasn't sure why. For breaking that terrible sense of panic in her? For releasing her tension?

She felt calmer and more able to cope when Sophy stirred, and even when the power suddenly failed. Not that it was really dark. It never got dark up here in summer.

'Something's brought the cable down,' he observed.

'Most likely a tree!' and she laughed.

'Why are you laughing?'

She looked surprised. 'I really don't know! Maybe it's the other side of the coin of despair . . . '

★ ★ ★

By the morning, the gale had blown itself out and an unreal calm lay over the havoc it had caused.

Along with the power line, a number of trees had been blown down and the ground was strewn with broken branches.

Keir's inflatable dinghy had disappeared from the beach and by mid-morning two anxious members of staff had arrived from the marine station in search of him. The dinghy had been found washed up on the Torquillan shore and they had realised — or hoped — that Keir had become stranded on the other side of the loch. Either that or he was *in* the loch.

As his rescuers loitered in the background, Keir awkwardly thanked Alison for her hospitality.

'It could have been a horrible night but it wasn't, thanks to you. In a weird way I enjoyed it!' he told her.

Alison blushed and lowered her eyes from his as she recalled that kiss and the comfort of his arms during the storm . . .

Apparently the new post-graduate student who was to work on the field station with Alison had arrived in Torquillan.

'I'll bring her over in the afternoon,' Keir told Alison as he left. 'And you'll be returning with me — so get packed.'

'No!' Alison said quietly but grimly. 'I haven't finished the work you assigned me here.'

His lips tightened — but then he managed a smile and a wave for Sophy as the engine roared and he was swept away.

It was late afternoon and the power had been restored when Keir returned with Alison's new assistant — a pleasant, brown-eyed girl called Meg. She immediately made friends with Sophy and fell in love with the abandoned seal.

The effects of being up all night were taking their toll on Alison. Her eyes were gritty and she felt almost sick with tiredness, and she asked her new companion if she would be kind enough to keep an eye on Sophy and Fairbairn while she rested.

Meg was delighted to take charge and Alison was astonished at the degree of relief she felt at being free to relax and leave everything in the hands of a competent team-mate.

As she snuggled down in the double berth, her eyelids already drooping, Keir McMaster was in her thoughts. Now her assistant had arrived, there was less need for him to visit the field station. How long would it be before she saw him again . . . ?

However, Keir continued to be a regular visitor. He appeared almost every evening during the following weeks, checking the oyster charts Alison was compiling and watching Fairbairn grow.

He seemed to take an inordinate interest in the seal's progress and planned to remove him to the marine station about mid-August.

As for Alison, she had begun to see a gentle side to his character — a side that showed he was a caring man, of whom she was growing very fond . . .

★ ★ ★

At Tigh na Mara, Sandy was missing Alison and Sophy more than he would have believed possible, and it wasn't helped by his sister's preoccupation with her own affairs.

She had had her friend, Kate Ogilvie, from Inverness to stay for most of July and they spent their time with their heads together, discussing their future house-sharing arrangements. It was Kate who had conceived the idea that, if they shared her house and split the outgoings, both would benefit. Then their pensions would stretch to more holidays and other treats.

The idea was very appealing to Peggy. Though Sandy picked up all the bills at Tigh na Mara, she didn't really enjoy village life and knew she would prefer the city. Yet still she dithered over it.

She had been sure that, if Sandy had his way, Bess Dunbar would be coming to live with them. But Bess didn't appear at all anxious to become Sandy's wife. Maybe, Peggy thought, she ought to wait and see . . .

Finally, Peggy opted to hedge her bets by deciding that she would move to Inverness for a trial period of three months and see how it suited her.

So it was that at the end of July, Sandy waved the two women off and turned back to the now empty house.

He would just have to get used to rattling around it on his own.

One morning a fortnight later, Sandy was mowing the front lawn when he was seized with such a longing to see Alison and Sophy that he left the mower where it stood and strode off to the garage to check the outboard motor.

His boat was anchored off the jetty in the village but he hadn't been out in it much recently.

He wondered if Bess would fancy the trip, and got as far as the telephone — but then he stood holding the receiver without dialling for a moment.

She'd been a wee bit shy with him since his proposal and hadn't come round at all when Peggy had had her friend staying. Maybe he'd rushed his fences?

Still, there was no harm in giving her a call, he persuaded himself, and slowly dialled her number.

'I'm going over to the other side of

the loch and up the lochan to see Alison and Sophy. How about coming?' he suggested.

'I can't, Sandy! My hands are covered in flour and I'm just putting scones in the oven,' Bess told him with a laugh.

'Scones are quick things.' His voice was hopeful.

'Yes, that's true,' she conceded.

'Well — I've still to go for the boat and row it back here to put the outboard on. Say — twenty minutes? Half an hour? Bring some of those scones — and don't forget the butter!'

He thought he heard her old, adorable gurgling laughter as he hung up and his heart lurched with pleasure.

He strolled along to the jetty, looking younger than his years in his blue jeans and a white shirt, deck-shoes and a jaunty yachting cap covering his greying hair. A little smile of happy anticipation played on his lips.

As he passed McDonald's Hotel, a white Mercedes drew up at the door and someone hailed him from the back seat.

'Captain Matheson! Sandy!'

As he turned in astonishment a vaguely familiar figure stepped out and his heart, so light just a moment ago, sank down into his deck-shoes.

He knew that thin, elegant form from the cruises!

He knew he should have replied to Mrs Ingersoll-Levine's warm letter. He should have written straight back saying he was engaged to be married to someone in Torquillan. But he hadn't. He'd been waiting to make his engagement to Bess a reality first.

'Mrs Ingersoll-Levine!' His heart sinking lower, he removed his cap, forced a smile to his lips, and stretched out his hand to her. 'I can hardly believe my eyes!' he said honestly.

'I hoped to surprise you, Sandy! But it's Ada, remember?'

He groaned inwardly. What am I going to do now, he wondered.

'I'm just rushing to take my boat

out.' He waved vaguely in the direction of the jetty. 'I've to meet a friend. How long are you staying?' He was shifting from one foot to the other.

'Ah, that depends,' she said archly. 'My plans are flexible.'

She turned away for a moment to instruct the driver to take her luggage into the hotel, and he seized the chance to glance around to see who might be witnessing this meeting. No one, thank goodness!

Mrs Ingersoll-Levine was gazing proprietorially at him again.

'When shall I see you then, Sandy? Dinner? Or I could come out in your boat with you. That would be fun!'

She grasped both his arms and he felt beads of perspiration form on his brow.

'It's just a wee dirty dinghy!' he exclaimed. 'We couldn't have you soiling your nice clothes coming out in it.'

Her white linen trouser suit was immaculate in spite of her journey and she was wearing rather a lot of gold jewellery.

'Well, dinner, then? I suppose I should check in now and perhaps have a rest before the evening.' She gave a little girlish giggle.

Sandy paused. He was caught between his desire to have the length of Scotland between them and his pride in the long tradition of Highland hospitality.

'I tell you what, Mrs — I mean, Ada. I'll come along here for dinner tonight, but you will be my guest. I don't have a cook at home at the moment.'

She released him and her right hand grasped her gold necklace in what appeared a spontaneous gesture of delight.

'Sandy! How lovely! And we can have a cosy chat at last! It's been so long . . . '

'Till tonight then.' He gave a smart naval salute and left her as quickly as he could.

When they were crossing the loch,

Sandy told Bess what had happened.

Bess frowned. 'But I thought you wrote putting her off . . . ?'

Sandy looked guilty.

'It was a good idea at the time but I found I couldn't tell a lie.' He looked at her appealingly. Bess had brought her granddaughter with her and the child's presence was inhibiting Sandy. 'Bess — Bess, would you come with me to the hotel tonight?' he pleaded.

'I'll do no such thing!' Her voice was unusually tart. 'How could I compete with a glamorous globe-trotter like that?'

'All right!' Sandy squared his shoulders. 'I'll deal with it when it happens. Right now the sun's shining, the breeze is fair — let's just enjoy ourselves. My, Sophy'll be pleased to see you, Helen! What a surprise we'll give her!'

He looked at Bess. When she'd come on board she'd been laughing and her eyes had been sparkling with fun. Now she looked put out, perhaps even upset.

That Mrs Ingersoll-Levine! He should

never have mentioned her. But Bess's daughter, Lorna, worked in reception at the hotel and she was bound to see Sandy with his dinner date. In any case, in a place the size of Torquillan, it was usually wiser to be open. You couldn't keep a secret round here!

★   ★   ★

Sophy saw the boat coming and raced down to meet it, her face alight with excitement. She couldn't wait to grab her friend by the hand and chase off with her.

Alison hugged her uncle and Bess with enthusiasm and peeped into Bess's basket, laughing while ushering them up to the caravan for tea.

'This is such a lovely surprise!' she kept repeating.

'My, you're looking grand, Alison. Isn't she, Bess?' Sandy exclaimed.

'You are indeed, dear!' Bess studied Alison. 'There's a completely different look about you. You've a lovely healthy glow and you look really relaxed!'

'That's good! This must rank with a Caribbean holiday! Who'd have thought?'

'You've been lucky with the weather,' Sandy agreed.

'Come and see our seal and meet Meg — she's been great company for us.' Alison smiled.

'Keir come over much?' Sandy asked casually as they walked.

'Most evenings,' Alison admitted and saw Bess's eyebrows arch in surprise. 'It's Fairbairn, the seal, he comes to see,' she added hastily then, to her horror, she felt herself beginning to blush.

She lengthened her stride so that she was leading them up the beach, following in the wake of the children.

* * *

Ada Ingersoll-Levine was still an attractive woman though, close to, one could see that her heavily made-up skin

217

was lined and her hair unnaturally black.

Her evening pants-suit was black, the top shot with silver lurex, and diamonds shone from her ears and fingers.

When she entered the hotel lounge, where most of those present were yachtsmen, regulars or holidaymakers, she struck a most sophisticated note. Heads were further turned when she rested her hand proprietorially on Sandy Matheson's arm.

When they were seated, Bess's daughter, going off duty after her spell on reception, came in to the bar and shot Sandy an astonished look when she saw him.

He felt guilty and wanted to go and explain himself to her, but Ada was demanding his attention.

As the meal progressed, after aperitifs and accompanied by a pleasant wine, Ada grew increasingly flirtatious, and the more exhausted Sandy became parrying her provocative remarks and drawing the conversation back to general topics, the more she slipped in her coy proposals.

'But you haven't told me when you're coming south to see me, Sandy!' She pouted. 'I've had your room prepared for months.'

Sandy felt his smile become fixed and he breathed deeply, wishing he was anywhere but here.

'Ada would like a little stroll after dindins,' she simpered, and Sandy stared at her. He'd forgotten about this childish act of hers. 'Sandy take Ada to his house for a nightcap later?'

In a flash Sandy realised how actively he disliked this woman. How different she was from Bess — how artificial.

At first he didn't recognise the woman when she appeared in the arched aperture that connected the dining-room with the lounge.

She didn't look like the Bess he knew. And yet — it was her! His heart did a complete somersault and he rose to his feet.

Her eyes were so blue — bluer than

he'd ever realised; larger, too. Her hair was freshly washed and set, gold earrings gleamed against her skin, and the soft cream of her stylish dress seemed to illuminate her complexion. She looked radiant.

'Ah — here's a friend of mine,' Sandy explained to his guest, stretching out an eager hand to Bess — though not at all sure what she was doing here.

He saw with relief that the twinkle was back in her eyes.

'Bess, meet a regular passenger from the old days on the cruise-liners — Mrs Ingersoll-Levine!'

'How do you do,' Bess said softly. 'It's a great pleasure to meet a friend of my fiancé.'

Having electrified them both, she sat down gracefully on the chair that Sandy had pulled out for her and looked blandly at each in turn.

Somehow Sandy managed to hide his astonishment as Ada turned startled eyes on him.

'You didn't mention that you're

engaged!' Her face had turned an unattractive red.

'Well . . . ' Sandy faltered, 'there was no occasion . . . ' He turned to Bess. 'You'll have coffee with us, dear, won't you?'

'Of course! How nice!'

As he signalled to the waiter, he was wondering what Bess was up to. Was this a joke — had she been put up to it?

'Do you mean to settle here permanently then, Sandy?' Mrs Ingersoll-Levine gave a nervous, high-pitched laugh. 'What on earth do you find to do all winter?'

Bess further astonished Sandy by now taking charge of the conversation. She replied pleasantly and entertainingly with a graphic account of winter gales and snow storms, gently interjecting tales of how the self-sufficient northerners entertained themselves.

'Well, it's been interesting,' Mrs Ingersoll-Levine remarked coolly when it was time to go and she was accompanying them to the door. 'If you don't mind I feel it's too late for me to take a walk with you now, Sandy,' she went on, before turning to Bess. 'I have to have an early night. I've to rejoin my friends at Speyside tomorrow, you see.'

'Oh, that's too bad,' said Bess, stretching out her hand. 'Perhaps we'll see you the next time you come north?'

'Such a surprise bumping into you today, Sandy!' Ada shook hands with both of them. 'I'm off on a three-month cruise in the spring — I'm not sure who the captain is going to be . . .'

But he'd better look out, Sandy thought.

⋆ ⋆ ⋆

He took Bess's arm unnecessarily firmly as they left and, without speaking, propelled her along the village street.

Half a mile beyond the houses they came to a seat that overlooked the water and he pressed her down into it.

'Well, lass?' he asked her huskily.

'Was that a game you were playing with me?'

Bess had lost her aplomb. She was exhausted — and distinctly nervous. Sandy looked grim. Had she got it wrong? Didn't he love her? What had come over her? She'd never behaved like that in her life before! Never fought for — for what she wanted . . .

'Well?' he pressed.

She couldn't make out the expression in his eyes. The August nights weren't so light. There was a glimmer on the water but the sky was dark, clouds closing in.

'It wasn't a game — well, not against you . . . ' she stumbled. 'I didn't know before . . . ' Her heart was pounding and she felt almost too breathless to get the words out.

'Didn't know what, Bess?' he asked gently.

She didn't answer but went on as though she was simply thinking aloud, trying to sort out her mixed-up thoughts and emotions.

'Not definitely. Not till this afternoon. I was shocked at myself — I felt so violently resentful that you were going out with another woman!'

'Bess! You mean . . . ?' He caught hold of her hands and tried to pull her to him but she resisted.

'No — wait a minute, Sandy. I've got to explain this, even if I'm making a fool of myself and you never want to see me again.'

'Bess!' He shook his head.

'It was this cruel pain. It was nothing but jealousy. I tried to suppress it and I thought I had till Lorna came home and described this glamorous creature on your arm.' Tears squeezed from under her lids. 'I'm so ashamed of myself.'

He caught her in his arms, not permitting her to pull away this time.

'There, there, mo ghaoil! There, there!' he gentled her but she wanted to tell him all that was on her mind.

He kissed her cheek as she turned her head away from him and struggled to find a handkerchief to dry her tears.

'When Lorna came in and described you and that lovely woman at the hotel together I thought, she can't have him — he's mine! Did you ever hear anything so awful?'

He chuckled. 'I never heard anything so marvellous in my life!'

'Och, Sandy! So you're not angry with me?' She felt her hand tightly squeezed and went on. 'All at once all my fears left me,' she admitted. 'My fear of change, my fear of making a fool of myself, of making a mistake, of annoying your sister, of deserting my son, though he's old enough to look after himself . . . Suddenly it didn't matter what anybody thought. I wanted you more than anybody's good opinion. And I'd left it too late!'

'Never!' he whispered, turning her face to him and pressing his lips down on hers.

'Oh, Sandy!' she whispered.

She didn't believe it could be happening to her — that lovely feeling of being in love. She snuggled against him, her heart full.

'I've been aching to kiss you for hours,' he said. 'You're the funniest wee thing I ever knew!'

'Oh, Sandy!' She gulped. 'Just where have my wits been?'

'I don't know — but thank goodness you've got them back! Maybe, if it hadn't been for Ada's visit, you never would have! Maybe I've something to thank her for after all.'

News At Last

The day Alison and Sophy returned to Torquillan, Fairbairn came, too. The seal wasn't too happy in his canvas sling but seemed pleased when he reached his new home. When he was lowered into the concrete pool at the marine station he proceeded to swim and gambol tirelessly to the delight of an admiring audience of station staff.

'He likes it!' Sophy clapped her hands with glee.

Like Alison, she looked tanned and healthy. The long summer weeks with so much of her mother's company had done a great deal to restore her sense of security and confidence.

'I should think he'll be strong enough to be returned to the sea in a month or so,' Keir McMaster pronounced.

'But he'll have to learn to catch his own fish and feed underwater first,'

Alison explained to her daughter.

Sophy would have to return to school soon, Alison realised. For that reason, she had been glad to leave Meg and another biologist at the field station and return to Torquillan to work on the data she had collected so far on the oyster project.

When Alison and Sophy got back to Tigh na Mara, both Sandy and Bess were waiting to greet them — looking very happy, Alison noticed.

'Sandy's got something to tell you,' Bess said.

'Bess and I are going to get married,' he announced happily.

'Uncle Sandy! Bess! That's the best news I've heard in ages!' Alison flew into her uncle's arms and then gathered Bess into a great big hug.

'Oh!' she exclaimed, wiping tears of surprise and joy from her eyes, 'I don't know when I was so glad about anything! There's a — there's a sort of glow about you both. I know!' Her eyes sparkled. 'We'll throw a party for you — an engagement party!'

'Wait till we buy the ring!' Sandy took Bess's hand.

'How about a fortnight on Saturday — just here at the house?' Alison suggested. 'I know how I want to arrange it — inside and outside too if it's a fine night. How will that do? Will you have shopped for the ring by then?' she asked excitedly.

'Yes.' Sandy grinned. 'We'll go to town this coming week. We'll have a great shopping spree, my love!' He placed his arm round Bess's shoulders, smiling happily.

Over the next two weeks, Alison got busy preparing and freezing as much of the party fare as could be done in advance. She had calculated that there would be somewhere between fifty and seventy guests, but she didn't want for help as Bess's daughter lent a hand and Marie and her aunt volunteered to do some catering, too.

She woke early on the morning of the party and dashed to look out of the window, the weather her first thought.

It was raining, but somehow it didn't worry her. Everything was organised and she felt relaxed, with an optimistic feeling that the sun would come out after the tide had turned in the afternoon.

Leaving Sophy still sleeping in the flat, she went down to her Uncle Sandy's kitchen to make a late breakfast for all of them.

She heard the postman at the front door and shuffled through to pick the letters, but even before she had lifted them up, she felt her mood inexplicably change and a strange premonition grip her heart.

She flipped through the envelopes and there among them was an official-looking one with a Kenyan stamp. It must be news about Clive!

Her hand was shaking as she laid the rest of the mail on the hall table and carried the envelope through to the kitchen and beyond, to the large larder.

She wanted to hide with it. She

didn't want anyone to see her face when she opened it. She was afraid of what it might contain . . .

The letter was from an official in Nairobi and informed her that an anti-poaching patrol had recently brought in two poachers. A wrist-watch had been removed from one of them, bearing what they suspected to be her husband's initials on the back.

When questioned, the man had sworn that the white man had been dead when they had come upon him — as a result of deadly snake-bite, they claimed. For their own reasons they had carried him some distance before burying him and placing a cairn over the body.

Convinced that the poacher was lying and that he or one of his companions had shot Clive, the police had had him lead them to the burial cairn, and exhumed the body to look for evidence of bullet wounds. They had found none — but they had found that the poachers had left the victim's gold wedding band bearing the inscription *A.McK.* to *C.E.*, and a date.

The body would be identified using dental records but there could be little doubt that it was Clive.

Alison felt as if her legs were about to fold beneath her.

The letter went on to request that some relative or friend travel to Kenya. There were formalities to complete, a funeral would have to be arranged . . .

I'll have to go, Alison realised, and her throat began to tighten against the nausea that threatened. But what about Sophy? How could she leave her, just when she was starting to gain confidence and settle down at last?

She groped her way back to the kitchen and sank on to a chair, trying to steady her teeming emotions.

She could hear her uncle padding about upstairs. He'd be down in a minute. He mustn't be allowed to guess what had happened until the party was over.

The party!

Somehow, through some super-human effort of will, she managed to keep a tight rein on her emotions and hid her feelings well as she prepared for the celebration.

She admitted to herself that she had come to terms with her loss since moving to Torquillan, had begun to make a new life for herself. But it was still a shock to receive this news confirming Clive's death.

How was Sophy going to react? She had seemed so happy recently. Would this news disturb her or had she already given up hope of seeing her father again?

Alison sighed. In a way it was a relief to hear what had happened. Now, at least, she could plan for the future — whatever that might hold.

The sun came out in the late afternoon as she had hoped it would and it shone, low and gold, long into the evening.

Everyone seemed to enjoy the party and Alison was happy for Bess and

Sandy. No-one could have guessed what she was going through or the dreadful news she had so recently received.

Exhaustion hit her about ten o'clock. She was out in the garden where most of the guests had drifted. At last it was getting darker and she flopped down on a bench facing the sea.

Marie, in a pink mini-dress with a beaded neckline, was engaging Keir in animated conversation nearby.

Alison watched them together for a few moments, hoping he would notice her. She felt in need of a friend — someone she could open her heart to, someone to comfort and support her. Odd that Keir should be the one she longed for . . .

She watched idly as a car drew up beside the wall at the bottom of the garden and a not unfamiliar figure emerged from it. She recognised Jim Muir, the oil engineer, Clive's former colleague and companion on that fateful safari. He'd probably got a communication about Clive too, and must have come to see her about it.

But she must just stop him coming into the garden and saying anything in front of the others — especially not where Sandy and Bess could hear. Not yet. Not tonight.

She rose and ran towards him, her fatigue forgotten.

★ ★ ★

'Can I get you some more wine?' Marie asked Keir.

'No, thank you. But shouldn't I be asking you that?'

'Oh, not tonight.' She giggled. 'You see, I'm a waitress tonight.'

'You're a waitress?' One dark eyebrow rose in that quizzical way that Marie found so devastating. 'I like your uniform!' He grinned.

Their laughter mingled with the noisy chatter around them but halted in surprise as Alison rushed past them down the footpath to the gate at the bottom of the garden.

They saw the dark silhouette of a man against the sea. They saw his hands stretch out to take Alison's which were flung towards him.

Keir's eyes were wide as he watched the man pull Alison into his arms and draw her head down to his shoulder, his hand caressing her hair.

There was a sharp crack beside Marie and she saw the stem and base of Keir's wine glass fall to the grass and unnoticed blood flow over his fingers. Her eyes went from the blood to the stark white angles of his face.

She lifted a thick paper napkin and pressed it into his hand, deftly removing the bowl of the glass as she did so.

Keir's face looked stricken as he watched Alison in the other man's arms.

★ ★ ★

Jim Muir had hesitated for a moment as he'd climbed out of his car. He'd had a hectic day and then driven fast from the east coast in an effort to reach Torquillan before nightfall.

Worrying all the time about his late colleague's wife, he'd been startled when he'd located her home to hear music, see lights blazing and a group of happy, chattering people outside on the lawn.

Perhaps she hadn't yet received the news about Clive from the Kenyan authorities . . .

'Jim!' He saw her running down the path towards him. 'You've had word, too!'

As she reached him, a well of gratitude and relief rose in her and filled her eyes with tears. Her hands reached out to him and he clasped them in sympathy and understanding that went beyond words.

The hardest part of the day had been the need to hide her emotions until the engagement celebrations were over. Now, for a moment, she could let go. The grief she felt over Clive's death was mixed with a strange relief that all the uncertainty was over.

Jim saw her distress and drew her into the comfort of his arms.

'It's all right. It's all right!' he murmured. 'Don't worry any more. It's past. It's over. I'm going to Kenya to attend to the formalities. I've been in touch with the authorities. They've agreed. It's all arranged.'

Incredulous, she looked up at him and gratitude deeper than she could ever express flooded her.

'Jim! I've never known of such kindness. I was dreading it. But, no — I can't let you. It's my responsibility.'

He shook his head. 'I always intended to if we ever got word. I want to. I consider it my duty to Clive — and to Clive's widow.'

Clive's widow! Alison shivered at his words.

She released herself slowly from the comfort of his arms, still looking up at him. He must have been making arrangements to go to Kenya all day, she realised, and then had obviously hurried to comfort her. What friendship!

'Come up, Jim, and have something to eat and drink. You must be shattered after driving all that way.'

She scrubbed the tears from her eyes with the backs of her hands and explained that the party was to celebrate her Uncle Sandy's engagement.

'I haven't told him about Clive — not yet. I didn't want to spoil his night. So, please, just for tonight, pretend there's nothing amiss. I'll tell my uncle in the morning. And then, there's Sophy.' Her hand clasped over her mouth. 'How shall I tell Sophy?'

'Look, you don't want me here just now, reminding you about it all. I'll go to the hotel in the village,' he said, 'and come over in the morning.'

'No, no! I'll make up a bed for you here. Please, Jim. I'm so grateful to you. I want you to stay. So will my uncle when he knows. It's a comfort to have you here. And then we can talk in the morning.'

They were making their way up the path as she spoke.

'To tell you the truth, I'm so tired I can hardly think, far less speak.' She pushed her hair away from her brow. 'We'll have to talk in the morning.'

As she casually introduced Jim to a group of her friends, she noticed that two people were missing. Keir had obviously left the party with Marie.

She was surprised by the emotion which filled her. She'd thought Keir was beginning to care for her, yet he'd gone off with Marie . . .

The surge of jealousy she felt threatened to shatter her brittle composure.

★ ★ ★

Marie threw herself energetically into her new life at drama college. She'd accepted the place she'd been offered soon after her audition but had kept, in a corner of her mind, the option of throwing everything up for the man she loved.

Now, though, she knew that there was no hope of Keir returning her love — that much had been patently obvious on the night of Bess and Sandy's party.

She'd kept her shoulders straight and her chin up then, and ever since. She didn't want anyone to guess how close she'd come to making a fool of herself, or that inside she was heartbroken.

Returning to the family home in Glasgow hadn't been easy either. Her sisters, Karen and Kirsty, were furious with her, for she'd got her old room back and they'd had to double up again.

Her father, meanwhile, couldn't understand how anybody would give up work to go back to school, as he called it.

'How did you get on at the school today, Marie?' he asked her as usual, eyeing his glamorous daughter quizzically.

'Fine, Dad — fine!' She wasn't going to let him know how much his teasing riled her.

They were round the table having their evening meal, but Marie was uncharacteristically quiet. Her own inner pain had had a curious effect on her. For the first time in her life she was becoming aware of other people's troubles.

She looked at her mother's plump, serene face and suddenly recalled her Aunt Isa's — in contrast, lined and filled with strain.

'Mum,' she said abruptly, 'poor Aunt Isa's ever so tired. She hasn't had a holiday for years — and she's had a busy summer.'

Her mother turned on her crossly.

'But you were sent up there to help her! And what did you do? You swanned off and took another job!'

This home truth would formerly have sent Marie storming out of the room, but not now.

'I know,' she said quietly. 'But you

said you would go up,' she continued. 'She's been looking for you all summer. Poor Isa!' She thought for an awful moment that she was going to burst into tears. 'It's a terrible thing,' she whispered, 'to wait and wait for somebody who never comes.'

'The lass is right,' her father agreed unexpectedly. 'You said you would go up, Mary.'

His wife shrugged uneasily.

'I know I did but I haven't got round to it yet, that's all. And,' she bridled, 'you'd think I had nothing to do here! Who's going to look after you lot?'

'You told Isa you'd send Karen or Kirsty if Marie left,' her husband continued.

'Yes, but I can't get either of them to go!' his wife snapped back.

Both girls kept their eyes on their plates.

'You could go and look after your mother for a month and give your sister a break,' Mr Blair told his wife. 'I'll tell you what I'll do,' he went on. 'I'll drive you up some weekend, and I'll even come back for you a month later.'

'But how will you manage?'

'Don't you worry about that — we'll manage. I'm sure I'll be fine with three daughters to look after me!' He smiled round at the three girls, then turned his attention back to his wife. 'Now, you go and phone your sister and tell her to arrange a holiday,' he ordered.

★　★　★

Just as Marie was settling into her new life, it was time for Fairbairn to try to learn some independence.

Although Alison had tried to prevent the little seal from mistaking her for his mother, he showed a decided partiality for her and had claimed a very special place in her heart. He had bravely clung to life against all the odds and she felt oddly proud of him.

As she'd fed him, day and night, he had rewarded her by gaining weight while his dappled fur had grown thick and glossy. Now he was as round as a little barrel, his knowing eyes bright and glowing.

She was proud of him but also a little ashamed, because Fairbairn was refusing to do any significant swimming without her. What would she do with him if he refused to go back to sea?

She couldn't even talk about it with Keir for he had been very offhand since the night of the engagement party. He was plainly avoiding her, and she was both hurt and confused.

They'd become friends over the long summer weeks when he'd taken such an interest in the seal pup, and she'd been sure that the attraction between them was — or had been — mutual.

So why had he left the party with Marie? What had happened to change his feelings towards her?

'You've got to learn to hunt to survive!' Alison told Fairbairn sternly as he flip-flopped awkwardly after her across the sand to the little bay below the station, then the wet-suited diver and the small seal took to the water.

Dim light, patterned by the wavelets, filtered down on to the white sand at the bottom. A little shoal of small fish fluttered past and Fairbairn was off in pursuit. Each day he was swimming farther and farther out. One day soon now, Alison was sure, he wouldn't return.

She slipped out of the water. She would take a stroll down in the afternoon to see if he'd gone.

So far, he had always been ready to come out and follow her home. Perhaps this would be the day that he wouldn't return. She'd spotted a curious seal farther out. Perhaps he'd make a friend.

★　★　★

She was later than usual in returning to the beach that afternoon because she'd had to attend a staff meeting.

Since Keir had begun to avoid speaking to her directly he chose to communicate in an impersonal manner during meetings and that afternoon, she had learned that he was going away.

'I'm going to Aberdeen for an unspecified time,' he told them. 'I'm to take part, as a visiting lecturer, in a marine-life programme. In the meantime, Mrs Evans will be in charge.'

'I will?' Alison asked, mystified.

'Naturally, since you're second in command. Unless you're moving to the east coast, of course,' he commented, then he moved swiftly on to other matters.

Infuriated, she caught up with him as he was striding off. In fact she stepped right in front of him to force him to stop and look at her.

'Just what did you mean by that remark?' she questioned him coldly. 'What did you mean about the east coast? Surely I'm not to be sent there?'

'Not sent. But that's where your oil engineer works, isn't it?'

She frowned. 'My oil engineer? What do you mean?'

'Jim Muir. Don't tell me you don't

know what I mean! I've seen for myself that he's very important to you.'

'Well, of course,' she agreed. 'He's the most incredibly kind . . . the most wonderful person I've ever known. He — '

But Keir didn't wait to hear. He turned on his heel.

'So I gathered,' he snapped before striding off.

Alison was almost glad when Fairbairn came flopping out of his pool to join her.

'Oh, Fairbairn, what am I going to do about that man!'

'That man' was driving out of the gate as they reached it. Seeing her with Fairbairn at her heels, he stopped the car and wound down the window.

'I've been watching the wild seal colony in the bay by the point. The mothers are leaving the pups for longer and longer periods by now.'

Whether it was an implied criticism of her or not, she took it as such and went white with indignation.

'Well, I'm following their example — aren't I? What do you think I've been doing all week?' And then her voice hardened. 'Why don't you try for a permanent post in Aberdeen when you're there!'

'I'm thinking about it,' he said coldly as he slid the car into gear and drove off.

On the next afternoon, when she came down to the shore, Alison saw Fairbairn's head bobbing in the water fifty yards out. She waited, expecting him to come ashore to her, but instead he did a few flips and a roll and then began to swim out of the little bay.

With an aching throat, Alison watched the silky black head glide farther and farther away towards the point where the seal colony was basking.

'Oh, Fairbairn . . . ' she sighed. 'I should be glad — but I wish I could call you back! Be happy, little seal. Be happy!' And she turned away with tears in her eyes.

Somehow she'd always imagined that Keir would be with her when Fairbairn was returned to the wild. She had grown accustomed to his companionship throughout the summer, although she'd tried to hide from herself how much she looked forward to his frequent visits, how pleased she'd been when she'd made him laugh. They'd become close — or so she'd thought.

Keir had laughed more and more as summer had progressed, laughed at Fairbairn lying on his back after Alison had fed him, his flippers folded over his tummy. And together they'd rejoiced in his every weight gain and the healthy shine in those friendly black eyes.

The small head could no longer be distinguished in the watery distance.

'Goodbye, Fairbairn,' she whispered softly, and she felt as though she was saying goodbye to so much more.

Love Is In The Air

Isa's sister, Mary, and her husband arrived on a Saturday. Karen had come with them for the run.

'I'll come back to Glasgow with you tomorrow, Dad,' she told her father.

'Well, I've said I'll take your aunt up to Inverness and then we'll go down the A9. Why don't you stay on with your mother for a wee while?' he cajoled.

'Not on your life!' was the uncompromising reply. 'I'm a Glasgow girl.'

Isa McPhail looked delighted to see them when she greeted the family at the door.

'The thought of having a break has fairly cheered me up!' she exclaimed, hugging her sister. 'Hello, John — and is this Kirsty or Karen?'

'I'm Karen, Aunt Isa. It's nice to see you.'

'My, you're like Marie — yet

different. With that black hair you're more like me. Come in and see your granny!'

'Have you got all your arrangements made, Isa?' Mary asked in the bustle of taking off coats and jackets.

'Oh yes. Over to Inverness for a day or two with my friends, then we're off, four of us, on a coach tour called Roman Britain. Then we've a week of shopping and sightseeing in York before coming north again. Oh, it'll be grand!' Isa smiled. 'But are you sure you'll manage all right, Mary?'

'Of course! We'll get on fine. Won't we, Mother?'

Her mother peered unrecognisingly at her.

'Who is it, Isa?' she asked querulously and Mary sighed.

'It's me — Mary. Your youngest daughter, remember? And this is John, my husband. Do you not remember him, Mother?'

Karen was looking out of the window with interest.

'D'you mind if I just go and explore a wee bit, Aunt Isa?'

'Not at all. You'll need your jacket, mind — there's a bit of a breeze blowing.'

'There sure is!' Karen sang to herself as she left the shelter of the village and hit the shore road. It's lovely, though, she thought, breathing in the fresh air.

In fact it was so blustery that, after a mile or so, she decided to turn back. The wind, coming behind her now, whipped her hair over her eyes and she pulled up the hood of her anorak and dug her hands into her pockets.

'Marie! Marie!' She heard a man's voice, deep and excited, shouting. 'Marie! Marie!' the voice bellowed again and feet could be heard pounding along the road behind her.

They came closer and a hand grasped her arm. She swung round, her hood falling back, and confronted the shocked face of the most handsome man she'd ever seen.

Deep colour ran up the tanned skin

to reach the tousled hair and surprise and embarrassment warred in the azure eyes.

'Oh, sorry! I thought you were Marie,' he said lamely.

'Actually I'm her sister, Karen. I'm just here for the weekend. Are you a friend of hers?'

It was a needless question. From the look of him he was another of Marie's conquests. Lucky Marie!

He couldn't take his eyes off her face.

'Her sister? Of course — I can see it now. You're so like her — and yet you're different.'

She wasn't wearing heavy make-up like Marie did and there was something attractively wholesome and natural about her. Her cheeks were rosy with the wind and her eyes dark and sparkling like her Aunt Isa's. Her smile was wide and unaffected and Gavin found his heart was racing.

She stared back at him, gazing deeply into his eyes, and for a moment time seemed to stand still.

Then they began to talk as he walked back with her to the village, and it was as if they had known each other for ever.

'Aunt Isa!' Karen spun into the house like a fresh spring breeze. 'Aunt Isa, I want to ask you something!'

'Yes, dear?'

'Could I stay here and learn about the post office work from you?' I'm good at maths and I'm good at organising things. Could I come here and live and help you with Gran, too?'

Isa smiled delightedly and turned to look at her sister and brother-in-law. John's jaw had dropped so far it was comical and Mary, who had been standing by her mother, collapsed into the nearest chair.

'Well I never!' she exclaimed.

'Who's this, now?' Mrs McPhail wanted to know.

'It's me — Karen, your granddaughter. You'll have to get used to me, Gran. You see, I'm going to be around for a long time!'

255

'What's brought this on?' Karen's father gasped.

'I've just met the man I'm going to marry!' she announced, and giggled gleefully.

'Does he know?' Her father was smiling.

'I don't think so, not yet. That's why I've got to stay!'

Isa shook her head and began to laugh and the old lady looked up at her questioningly.

'Who did you say she was?' she quavered.

'It's your granddaughter, Karen — Marie's sister. You remember Marie?' Isa continued to laugh. 'Marie was good fun, Mother. But this one'll be the end of us!' And she wiped the tears of laughter from her eyes.

*   *   *

Alison kept telling herself how lucky she was. The people who'd rented her house in Colchester were keen to buy it and she'd left everything in the hands of her solicitors.

Sophy seemed happy at last. She hadn't seen her father for so long that she had accepted the news of his death fairly philosophically. There had been tears when Alison had explained that she would never see him again, but her grieving was soon over.

Meanwhile, having worked a twelve-hour day since Keir had left, she felt she was really on top of the job now. She got on well with the rest of the staff and they all worked in harmony.

All in all, she had everything she wanted in life — so why was she still so unhappy?

Finally she admitted to herself that it was because of Keir McMaster. She was missing him; she couldn't get him out of her mind. But hadn't he made it plain that he preferred Marie's company?

However, she soon heard from Gavin that Marie was at college in

Glasgow — and that Keir hadn't visited her there.

Alison smiled. Poor Gavin — trying so hard to pretend that he wasn't smitten with Marie's sister, Karen; that he hadn't finally met his match. But she could see his heart was lost.

We'll not be seeing so much of him in the future, she thought forlornly.

The ringing of the phone broke into her thoughts. She heard Sophy answer it and then the girl called, 'Mum! It's for you — it's Mrs Craig!'

'Mrs Craig?' Alison whispered, puzzled, trying to place the name, and took the phone.

'Mrs Evans? It's Mrs Craig — Dr McMaster's housekeeper.'

'Oh hello, Mrs Craig! Of course — how are you?'

'I'm fine, thank you. I'll tell you why I'm phoning. Could you come up? There's a cat here which might be Sophy's. I think the cold has driven it off the hill. There are two kittens, too — the remains of a litter I think. They're all a bit poorly . . . '

'We'll come right away, Mrs Craig. Thank you very much for phoning.'

Alison put the receiver down, a broad smile on her face. Sophy's cat had been lost in the hills so long ago that she had given up hope of it ever being seen again.

'What is it, Mummy? I don't want to go out! It's too cold — and anyway, I'm watching the cartoons!'

'Darling, I don't know if it's fair to tell you yet, but Mrs Craig thinks she may have Tabitha there,' Alison said tentatively.

Sophy's eyes grew round as saucers.

'Tabitha!' she breathed. 'Oh, Mummy!'

'Try not to get too excited, pet. It might *not* be her,' she warned her. 'After all, Mrs Craig has never seen her before.'

'Oh, but I do hope it is!'

★ ★ ★

In spite of her warning words, they were both excited by the time they parked in the yard behind Keir's house. They found the back door open, knocked and walked in.

'Are you there, Mrs Craig?' Alison called.

But it wasn't Mrs Craig who was waiting for them in the kitchen, it was Keir McMaster.

Alison froze, remembering his distant treatment of her before he'd left. Her eyes were cold as she regarded him.

He held up his hands in a gesture of defence.

'I owe you ten thousand apologies. I had to talk to you.'

'Where's Mrs Craig?' Alison demanded.

'Tabitha!' Sophy squealed joyfully, hurrying over to the stove and kneeling down beside a basket there.

'I asked Mrs Craig to phone you and not mention my name. I recognised Tabitha from seeing her at your uncle's house.'

'I thought you were in Aberdeen.'

Alison bristled and turned away to watch Sophy.

The child was staring down at her beloved Tabitha and the two skinny kittens. Tabitha had lost her plump good looks. Life had obviously been hard for her on the hill.

'Don't touch her yet, Sophy,' Keir advised. 'She's still a bit wild. I thought I heard a cat crying out in the yard when I got back today and my cat was indoors,' he explained. 'Poor Tabitha — she was looking for shelter and food, forced down from the hill by the snow, I expect.'

'Oh, poor Tabitha!' Sophy's fingers hovered over her friend, longing to touch her. 'And, oh, Mummy! Look at the kittens!'

'I think they're still taking milk from their mother and that's weakened her dreadfully. I've been trying to get them to lap,' Keir said.

Alison was happy to see the cat back, especially for Sophy's sake.

'Mrs Craig is through in the lounge

with Sheba, our cat — who objected strongly to the others coming in, Sophy!' Keir had trouble gaining her attention. 'Would you mind if I took your mum away for a little while? I'd like to talk to her.'

Sophy, totally absorbed in her little cat family, paid little heed.

'Alison, would you you mind coming through?' She'd never heard him sound so tentative.

They went through to the lounge and Mrs Craig left them alone and came bustling into the kitchen, chatting to the child as she set about her chores.

'Dr McMaster was sure it was your cat, pet. Are you pleased to see her? Now, I'll just get organised. I've to make tea for us all in half an hour.'

★ ★ ★

'Please sit down,' Keir invited Alison awkwardly, although he seemed unwilling to do so himself and kept pacing about the room.

Alison remained standing. She didn't care to sit and have him towering above her. What was this all about anyway?

Finally he paused by the window and looked out while she stood with her back to the fire, grateful for its warmth. She got the feeling he was trying to figure out the best way to say whatever it was he had to tell her.

Suddenly he spoke again.

'I met your friend Jim Muir in Aberdeen.'

She stayed silent, sending him a look of cold disdain as she remembered their last exchange before he'd left.

He swung round and faced her.

'You knew he had a wife there?' he added.

She kept her face expressionless, her voice cold and steady, as she replied, 'Wife and children, permanent home, the children's schools.'

'But you're on terms of intimacy with him?' he pressed.

'Hardly!' She sounded weary. 'He's been so kind — more than a friend.'

Why should she try to explain to him all that Jim Muir had done for her?

Four strides brought Keir across the room to her.

'Why was he holding you in his arms?' he demanded.

'To comfort me.' She shrugged coolly in spite of the turmoil within her. 'You wouldn't let me explain . . . '

'You should keep out of his arms unless — '

'Don't be absurd!' Her voice was low. 'You're acting like a jealous lover when it's all too clear that nothing could be further from the truth. If you cared for me you wouldn't have ignored and humiliated me the way you have.'

Her gripped her shoulders and stared down into her eyes.

'I'm sorry. I do love you. I love you so much it's eating me up!'

He searched her expressive eyes and saw weariness and sadness there. She was too pale and thin, her skin almost transparent.

This was too much for her. She

shrugged out of his grasp and sank down on the fireside chair and, after a moment, he took the seat opposite and leaned towards her, remorse for having added to the strain he saw in her consuming him.

'I never thought I would feel like this again,' he admitted slowly. 'But you got to me. The last time I saw you, with Fairbairn, you were so defiant and beautiful, so sad and tender — you nearly broke my heart!' He looked at her, a frown now lining his forehead. 'Why was Jim Muir comforting you?' he couldn't help asking.

She let out a long sigh and started to tell him what had happened and all Jim Muir had undertaken on her behalf.

'Not only did he do all that,' she concluded, 'but he's arranging a funeral for Clive and a plaque, so that if ever Sophy wants to find her father's grave . . . ' She shook her head. 'I can never repay the debt I owe him.'

He was silent for a long time before he spoke.

'Why couldn't you have shared this with me that night?' he asked, leaning forward to touch her pale cheek with a gentle finger.

'Don't you see? I didn't want a breath of it to spoil Uncle Sandy's party. I saw Jim arrive and I ran to meet him to stop him coming up and saying anything. Then I got a bit emotional. I'd been so strung up all day, and he just held me till I calmed down.' She smiled wistfully at Keir and he felt his heart start to race.

'Will you marry me, Alison?' His voice was pleading and she trembled a little at the look in his eyes, but she shook her head, memories of her unhappy marriage filling her mind.

'I'll never marry again,' she said decisively.

To her surprise he nodded in evident understanding.

'I knew that you'd been hurt,' he said gently. 'Was it bad?'

'Bad!' She sniffed. 'Endless humili-ation, being put down, belittled, criticised — till all my confidence was gone.'

'And you've been fighting ever since to build it up again?' he asked gently.

'Like a tiger!' She laughed at herself.

'And I gave it a swipe with my bad behaviour,' Keir realised.

Again there was that rare perception she had seen in him before, and it made her look at him with sympathy.

'You've been hurt before, too. Your divorce — '

He nodded.

'Yes. It made me wary of starting any new relationships — scared of my feelings for you,' he told her quietly. 'I thought if I went away . . . But I couldn't get you out of my mind. I adore you. I adore your aggression, your self-sufficiency — and your vulnerability. It's a devastating combination!'

She laughed shakily, avoiding his eyes.

'I want to be independent.'

'I know that.' His voice was soft,

understanding. 'You'll need time to learn to trust me. But perhaps in the spring you'll feel differently. I can wait,' he said simply.

His gentle words touched her heart.

'I was hurt, too,' he continued. 'And embittered. But I see now that we mustn't spend our lives looking back. I never imagined I could feel like this again.'

His face broke into a transfiguring smile, bringing a rueful grin to hers.

'I grew to love you with all my heart this summer,' he went on. 'And I care for Sophy, too. You'll always matter to me — to the end of my life. D'you think you could consider my proposal? Could you learn to love me?'

'Maybe in the spring,' she agreed, and saw him smile.

'Could we seal that bargain with a kiss?'

He pulled her to her feet and gave her a brief, light kiss, but she moved into his arms and lifted her lips as his mouth touched hers again. How long could she deny her feelings for him? If only she could free herself from the fear of giving her heart again.

His kiss was passionate yet gentle and she was trembling when he pulled away.

'Oh, Keir!' Softness and indecision came to her face. 'I can't think when you do that!'

'Good,' he said. 'I'm going to keep on doing it till you agree to marry me.'

They were interrupted by a call from Mrs Craig.

'That's the tea ready now, Dr McMaster!'

'Right! We're coming through to have it with you and Sophy in the kitchen. Be there in a minute,' he called back.

He turned back to Alison.

'Sophy's a lovely girl, Alison. She helps ease the painful memories of the child I lost . . . ' His eyes misted and the muscles at the corners of his mouth quivered.

He pulled Alison, unresisting, down on to the settee and took her in his arms. They gazed at one another in silence.

Keir's kisses had brought the old longing for him surging back, but now a passionate tenderness overwhelmed her. She pushed back a lock of his hair with gentle fingers.

'Do you love me?' he probed.

She looked away, avoiding his eyes, but he had seen a flash of the answer he wanted.

'There's no escape you know,' he murmured. 'There'll never be anyone else but you. I'll wait — for ever if necessary . . . '

'Maybe it won't be necessary,' she whispered, lifting her face to his, love shining in her eyes.

They had kissed before, but this time when their lips met the kiss they shared held a world of promises for the future.

We do hope that you have enjoyed reading this large print book.

Did you know that all of our titles are available for purchase?

We publish a wide range of high quality large print books including:
Romances, Mysteries, Classics
General Fiction
Non Fiction and Westerns

Special interest titles available in large print are:
The Little Oxford Dictionary
Music Book, Song Book
Hymn Book, Service Book

Also available from us courtesy of Oxford University Press:
Young Readers' Dictionary
(large print edition)
Young Readers' Thesaurus
(large print edition)

For further information or a free brochure, please contact us at:
Ulverscroft Large Print Books Ltd.,
The Green, Bradgate Road, Anstey,
Leicester, LE7 7FU, England.
Tel: (00 44) **0116 236 4325**
Fax: (00 44) **0116 234 0205**

Joanna Baxter flies from Sydney to run her parents' small farm in the Adelaide Hills while they recover from a road accident. But after crossing swords with Riley Kemp, life is anything but uneventful. Gradually she discovers that Riley's passionate nature and quirky sense of humour are capturing her emotions, but a magical day spent with him on the coast comes to an abrupt end when the elegant Greta intervenes. Did Riley love Greta after all?

SUMMER IN HANOVER SQUARE

Charlotte Grey

The impoverished Margaret Lambart is suddenly flung into all the glitter of the Season in Regency London. Suspected by her godmother's nephew, the influential Marquis St. George, of being merely a common adventuress, she has, nevertheless, a brilliant success, and attracts the attentions of the young Duke of Oxford. However, when the Marquis discovers that Margaret is far from wanting a husband he finds he has to revise his estimate of her true worth.

CONFLICT OF HEARTS

Gillian Kaye

Somerset, at the end of World War I: Daniel Holley, unhappily married to an ailing wife and father of four grown-up children, is attracted to beautiful schoolteacher Harriet Bray, but he knows his love is hopeless. Daniel's only daughter, Amy, who dreams of becoming a milliner and is caught up in her love for young bank clerk John Tottle, looks on as the drama of Daniel and Harriet's fate and happiness gradually unfolds.